THE

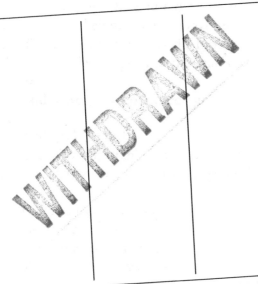

Point

THE HIGHEST FORM OF KILLING

Malcolm Rose

Good to meet you

Malcolm Rose

Scholastic Children's Books,
Scholastic Publications Ltd,
7–9 Pratt Street, London NW1 0AE, UK

Scholastic Inc.,
555 Broadway, New York, NY 10012-3999, USA

Scholastic Canada Ltd,
123 Newkirk Road, Richmond Hill,
Ontario, Canada L4C 3G5

Ashton Scholastic Pty Ltd,
P O Box 579, Gosford, New South Wales,
Australia

Ashton Scholastic Ltd,
Private Bag 92801, Penrose, Auckland,
New Zealand

First published in 1990 by André Deutsch Limited

This edition by Scholastic Publications Ltd, 1994

Text copyright © Malcolm Rose 1990

ISBN 0 590 55536 7

Typeset by TW Typesetting, Midsomer Norton, Avon
Printed by Cox and Wyman Ltd, Reading

10 9 8 7 6

So Abram rose, and clave the wood, and went,
And took the fire with him, and a knife.
And as they sojourned both of them together,
Isaac the first-born spake and said, My Father,
Behold the preparations, fire and iron,
But where the lamb for this burnt-offering?
Then Abram bound the youth with belts and straps,
And builded parapets and trenches there,
And stretched forth the knife to slay his son.
When lo! an angel called him out of heaven,
Saying, Lay not thy hand upon the lad,
Neither do anything to him. Behold,
A ram, caught in a thicket by its horns;
Offer the Ram of Pride instead of him.

But the old man would not so, but slew his son,
And half the seed of Europe, one by one.

                                    Wilfred Owen

In no future war will the military be able to
ignore poison gas. It is a higher form of killing.

                                    Fritz Haber
                        1919 Nobel Prize speech

Chapter 1

The blue Escort rolled down the track between the dunes, lurching to a stop before it ran onto the soft sand of the beach. A man staggered out of the car. "Come on!" he shouted back into the car.

"But we haven't got costumes. Or towels."

"Who needs them? There's no one about. And it's not cold. We'll soon dry off. Come on, Ellen, I'll race you."

"No chance! It might feel lovely and warm here but the water won't. It's April, Jack, and this," Ellen indicated the beach, "isn't the Costa del Sol. It's Devon."

Jack peered out to sea, and then said through the open window, "Looks okay to me – no icebergs."

Ellen grinned and shook her head. "I'm too full

of booze for swimming and racing. Besides," she added, "it's Thursday tomorrow and I have to be at work early."

"Spoil sport!" Jack walked round to Ellen's side of the car and opened her door. Offering her his hand, he said, "Let's go for a quick paddle instead, then."

As they kicked off shoes and removed socks and tights, Ellen said, "This is a mad idea, Jack."

"But all my best ideas *are* mad ones." Jack rolled up his trouser legs and Ellen giggled at the sight. "Very sexy!" she said.

"Aren't I always?" Jack took her hand and impelled her into a trot towards the sea.

The moon hung low in the sky and, like a beacon, cast a thin shaft of light over the calm sea into the bay. The beam was finally scattered where the waves rippled up onto the seashore. At the water's edge, Ellen hesitated. "It *is* cold."

"Rubbish!" Jack shouted as he dashed into the sea, splashing water all around him. He stopped when the water reached his knees, then turned to Ellen. "Come on. It's great."

"Well, refreshing anyway," Ellen gasped as she trod gingerly towards him on tip-toe.

Jack put his arm around his wife's shoulders and squeezed. "You look marvellous tonight. Good party?"

"Mm. Very good." They kissed.

"You know," Jack said, "in all the best films the hero does wonderful things with the heroine in shallow water."

"Is that just before he gets eaten by a shark?"

"You've got the wrong film there."

"And you've got the wrong climate!" They laughed and together began to wade along the seashore. "What's that?" Ellen asked, pointing to a dark lump amongst the breakers some distance ahead of them.

Jack shrugged. "A stump of a tree? I don't know. Maybe it's a courting couple."

Ellen elbowed him. "Oh, shut up. It's probably that shark!"

"Too small," Jack retorted.

As they approached the object, it was Ellen who recognized it first. In revulsion and shock, she cried out, "Jack!"

"All right, Ellen. All right. It's a dog. Just a dog."

"Yes, but look at it!"

"I know. I'll get it to the beach."

"Don't touch it, Jack."

"And just leave it here? It might get washed away. No, I'll get it out."

He decided that a leg was the least distasteful part to touch so he took hold and dragged the body to the shore. The flesh was soft and clammy with the water, but the body was rigid. He pulled it out onto the beach where even in the semi-darkness he could see the full extent of the dog's injuries. Where it had lost its hair the body was oddly yellow, as if horribly diseased and lacking in blood. The bone on one side of its head was clearly visible. Jack turned and emptied the contents of his stomach onto the sand.

Ellen's eyes flicked between the dog and Jack. "What. . . ?"

Suddenly sober, Jack interrupted. "I don't know. But there's something wrong." He wiped his mouth and thought for a moment. "Look, I'll stay here and keep an eye on it. You go off and get the camera."

"Camera?"

"Yes. In the car. Something's not right here, Ellen. I think we've got to tell the police. But," he said, "I want a record of it before we phone them. Tell you what, it's not that dark so I won't lose it if I go and get the camera. I'll take a photo of it while you go and call the police. I think there's a phone box by the main road. If not, there's a house over there – further along the front."

Jack took two shots of the dog's body, from different angles, then went to wait out of its sight in the car. As he pulled his trousers away from his uncomfortably wet legs, he muttered to himself. "Yes, it was a mad idea." The extraordinarily warm April night had suddenly turned chilly.

Ellen returned and sat by his side in the car. She

wanted desperately a palatable explanation for the dog's appearance, even though she knew that there could not be one. "What do you think did that to it? Fish? Or just the water?"

"No chance. No fish ever did that. Something strange did it." He took Ellen's hand. "I'm sorry, love."

"It's not your fault." Ellen smiled. "It's been a marvellous evening anyway."

There was no siren to herald the approach of the police, just headlights glaring. Jack and Ellen got out of the car. "Three cars! What did you tell them, Ellen? That we'd discovered a mass murderer? Hang on . . ." Jack's eyes screwed up. "They've stopped up the road. And they're not police cars."

Ellen edged nearer to her husband. "What are they?"

"Two vans and a jeep. Hell. Look."

Men were pouring out of the vehicles, torches flashing and panning. All of the men were dressed entirely in white, as if in space-suits.

"Jack?"

"I don't know, Ellen. I don't know. Some sort of protective gear."

The strings of light spread out as they approached, obviously intending to cast their luminescent net around the area.

"Ellen," Jack whispered. "Reach into the car. Slowly. Pass me the camera."

"Okay." The back window was wound down so Ellen simply reached in and plucked the camera off the back seat where Jack had left it. "Here," she said.

Jack held it behind his back as a flashlight caught him in its beam. "Damn." The beam was kept on him. "Get that light off me," he muttered. Noiselessly the white figures were getting closer and closer, and the torch-light remained on him.

"Do something, Jack."

He nodded, took a step forward and shouted, "The dog's down there, not here!" As he pointed, he stepped out of the light and threw the camera as far as he could into the dunes.

Four of the men approached Jack and Ellen, the rest spread out over the beach. "Just stay where you are. We'll deal with the dog."

"What's going on?" Ellen asked.

"Never mind about that. Just tell us, are there just the two of you?" The voice from behind the anonymous mask was muffled and mixed with slight hissing noises from the air cylinder strapped to the man's back.

"Yes."

"And have you contacted anyone besides the police?"

"No," Jack replied.

"You phoned, didn't you?" The man addressed Ellen. "Did you see or contact anyone else?"

"No."

"Did you touch the dog?"

"No," Ellen answered.

"Any close contact at all?"

"Well, yes, in the sea . . ."

The voice interrupted her, turning to Jack instead. "You?"

"Yes," Jack said. "I brought it ashore."

"Okay," the man spoke to his colleagues, "take him in your van. We'll take the woman."

"Wait a minute!" Jack cried. But it was no use. He was being held back by the arms as Ellen was bundled away. The separation was all so sudden. He could not even reply when Ellen shouted back over her shoulder, "Jack!"

Jack never saw his wife again. As he was being led away himself, only two thoughts comforted him. Perhaps they wouldn't spot the camera. And he knew his wife's voice well enough to know that she had lied to her captors. She *had* spoken to someone else.

Chapter 2

Thursday April 15th
I wonder how it happens. A sudden impulse?
A well thought out plan, painstakingly executed? It
all seems too important a step to be decided on a
whim, but could I sustain the courage for longer
than a split-second? I doubt it.

Next year I'll be replaced by a robot arm. All day I
sit preparing samples and loading them into the
magazine. Already the analysis runs itself overnight. When the arm is perfected, there'll be no
need for me at all. The robot will do a better job
too. It won't make mistakes. Sampling is always
perfect, reproducible. It wouldn't have to wear the

gear like me. It won't care about toxicity. And it won't have a conscience.

But there we have it. It's not unemployment that really bugs me, it's employment.

Chapter 3

It was Friday and really too warm for much walking but Derek felt that he had no choice. He stopped, stretched and threw the stone in his hand into the sea. At least it was better than sitting brooding in his office. He had put three miles behind him already that morning but he didn't know how many were in front. He didn't even know what he was looking for. He hoped that it would be obvious when he found it. He slung his jacket over his shoulder and trudged on.

His hope was realized within half an hour's walk. The beach was fenced off, the small wooden sign read simply, "Beach Closed. Unexploded Bomb." A policeman on the other side of the barricade strolled towards him. In deep Devonian tones, the policeman said, "We still keep finding 'em."

"A bomb?"

"Aye. The irony is that it's probably one of ours. When I was a lad they trained all over this coast, using live ammunition."

"Have they dealt with it yet?"

"Yes, the one that was found is safe. They're searching in case there's others." He jerked his thumb in the direction of a dozen men some way along the beach.

"Metal detectors?"

"Guess so."

Derek nodded. At a distance it was difficult to decide. They could have been metal detectors but it looked more as if the men were spraying the beach. And they were wearing some form of protective gear with breathing apparatus.

"Well, sir . . ."

"Yes," Derek said. "I'll turn back. Any idea when it'll be open again?"

The policeman grunted derogatorily. "Not as quick as it would be at the height of the season. The council would really put a bomb under them then."

Derek drove over to the other side of Crookland Bay where the cliffs rose, grey and ribbed. He parked his car by the cones that marked the site of Wednesday night's crash. Ellen's car had smashed through the metal barrier, bounced down the cliff and now lay like a stranded fish on the rock below. Only a black twisted skeleton remained. Derek sighed and thought back to the explanation that he'd been offered by the police that morning. "They'd been to a party, you see. Apparently, Mr Banks had had a lot to drink. It's a nasty twisting road, that cliff road." Derek looked down at the wreck and thought of his sister. Mischievous, pretty, insecure. "Yes, a horrible accident. Nothing could be salvaged from the car, I'm afraid. Neither bodies nor possessions. The heat would have been terrific." Derek looked down at the wreck and realized that he was out of his depth. The police chief's voice that droned in his head was telling him such a different story from the one that Ellen had hastily poured out over the telephone. She'd said that she had called the police out to the beach. The chief hadn't even mentioned that telephone call and had referred only to the site of the crash on the cliff road. And there was certainly nothing about a dead animal. The chief's version of events was so inconsistent with Ellen's that it stank of some sort of weird cover-up. Derek stood on the cliff top and wondered if he would have got the same story from the police if he'd admitted that Ellen had called him too. But he hadn't challenged the police story because, if some grand conspiracy was afoot, he didn't want to alert them to his suspicions.

Derek realized why Ellen had phoned, of course. She needed support and reassurance, and normally

Jack provided it. But when her intuition told her that they had stumbled across something that made Jack as helpless as she was herself, she turned to her brother. Derek was used to it. He knew that to Ellen he was a model of coolness and intelligence. An oracle. Now he saw his reputation collapsing as he looked over the cliff and saw painted onto the sand Ellen's imploring face – an afterglow of whatever had befallen her. Derek felt that he must find out what had really happened but had little idea how to go about it. Certainly he could not turn to the police. At that moment, his self-imposed compulsion to discover the truth seemed a heavy burden. He could so easily let Ellen down. And because of that he felt guilt. It added to the guilt that he already felt through telling her, in that phone call in the dead of Wednesday night, that there was probably nothing to worry about.

Of course, it had crossed his mind that Ellen was drunk. Drunk and mischievous. She phoned as a prank, then afterwards they crashed the car. Just as the police claimed. But Derek didn't believe it. Even on a bad line, he could distinguish Ellen's impish voice from her vulnerable one. He had heard only uncertainty and alarm. Anyway, her story was too far-fetched to be merely a prank.

It was getting late. Too late to drive two hundred miles home. Instead, he drove back into town, to the bed-and-breakfast district. Row after row of boarding houses, all the same. He chose one at random. The landlady, as round and as jovial as a picture postcard stereotype, showed just a hint of suspicion of a tourist with next to no baggage wanting a room for one night only. She took his money anyway and directed him to his room. "At least you should get a decent night's sleep. Not woken up at the crack of dawn by helicopters," she said.

"Helicopters?"

"Aye. Earlier this week we were plagued with them. Some training exercise, I suppose. As soon as the sun was up. But they stopped a day or two back."

Helicopters or not, Derek did not sleep. He was comfortable enough but his head was full of thoughts. Questions with no answers. Like an equation with too many unknowns. He didn't really know if the closed beach had anything to do with Ellen and Jack. It was just an assumption. But if he was short of facts, what could he do to solve the equation but make assumptions? If he was right, the unexploded bomb was just a cover. Presumably for something more sinister. Something from which the public was excluded, protected. And, whatever it was, it necessitated protective suits from head to toe. Of course, he could get dressed and creep down to the beach to look for clues like some daring, furtive schoolboy. But what good could it do? If the authorities were so concerned about something on the beach, all traces would have been removed by now. Besides, if it was so dangerous it would not help to jeopardize himself. Look what happened to Ellen and Jack.

What had happened to Ellen and Jack? The beach would not reveal anything so what could? There was one item which, if found, would disprove the police story. Ellen said that Jack was going to photograph the dead dog. Derek would love to get his hands on that camera. According to the police, though, it would be just a pile of ashes by now. There again, he was sure that the police had faked the accident at the cliff, so perhaps the camera wasn't burnt at all. It was most likely that the authorities had it. There was just a chance, though, that Ellen had managed to ditch it before they seized it. Derek could not question the police about the camera without revealing that he knew more than he cared to admit. He realized that finding the camera was a real long shot, even if Ellen and Jack had somehow conspired to keep it from the police. It could be anywhere. Despite this, it was too important to discount. In the morning, before driving home, he visited the offices of the local newspaper. Derek knew that he was clutching at straws but, just in case, he placed an advert for the camera in the Lost and Found. He wasn't sure why, but he used a false name.

Chapter 4

Friday April 16th

Chemistry's been my life. Sounds pathetic, doesn't it? But there we are. Nine "O" levels in an all-boys' school. Into the sixth-form. Maths, Physics and Chemistry. Straight from "A" levels to university. That's where I saw girls for the first time. But I had no time for them – there was a compulsion for me to learn everything I could about chemistry. In those days the degree had to be a good one to stand any chance of a job. Well, it paid off, didn't it? I got a job all right.

So, you see, I've never had a girlfriend. I know them well enough, know what makes them tick. We're all little bags of chemicals, after all. I know their normal state, their pregnant state, their diseases. They are readily characterized. But happiness and love . . . Those I don't know. They're not so easily defined – just a bit more adrenalin being pumped around. In fact, all emotional states are difficult for me. I can't quantify them.

Chapter 5

It was one o'clock, Saturday morning. Mark, unable to sleep, gazed out of his bedroom window. A peaceful night. He could not even hear the sea. It was as calm as it had been on Wednesday night when he'd also been too restless to sleep. Then, his mind had been occupied with questions about Sylvia, and how she had grown away from him. He'd thought of her a lot since October. As soon as she'd accepted the place at the university up in the Midlands, he just knew that he was in danger of losing her. Yet being aware of the danger hadn't made it any easier for him. It had only accentuated his pain and anger at their enforced separation. She'd been back in the area for two weeks now and he'd been virtually ignored by her.

Just one lousy date – or get-together as Sylvia had preferred to call it. Why was she so cold towards him? Had she found someone else at college?

His thoughts had been interrupted by activity far along the beach. He had seen the headlights of a car in the second before they were extinguished. Inquisitively, he'd reached for his binoculars and just made out a couple of midnight revellers frolicking on the beach. When the couple emerged from wading in the sea, the woman dashed up Bocking Lane and was there, out of Mark's sight, for a good few minutes. Mark hadn't been able to see what the man did in the meantime. It was shortly after the woman returned that the rumpus really began, like some candle-lit ritual. The revellers were surrounded by a dozen or so torch-bearing figures, then marched away. Their car was driven off and the beach closed. He didn't believe for one minute that there had been a bomb. You don't get dozens of men trampling over a beach with a suspected unexploded bomb around. And ever since Wednesday night, the helicopters had stopped their all-day searches of the coastline. Mark did not believe in coincidences either.

Mysteries always kept him awake. On Wednesday the mystery of Sylvia had haunted him and led him to the mystery that kept him awake tonight. Just what was going on down on Crookland Bay's beach? Mark shook his head irritably. There was only one thing for it. He grabbed his torch and, with a tingling spine, crept downstairs and into the lounge. This room, directly below his bedroom at the back of the house, provided an ideal and well used escape route to the beach. The patio door slid open quietly and he stepped out into the small garden. A gate led from the garden straight onto the dunes. He made his way towards the site of Wednesday's commotion. What was he hoping to find there? An explanation, of course.

The night was cool and quiet. Eerie. Perfect. He scanned the beach for policemen. There did not seem to be any around so he vaulted over the barricade onto the prohibited shore and lit his torch. Head down and eyes screwed up, he scoured the sand. The flashlight picked out a discarded crisp packet, seashells, a flattened can. Nothing. Had he risked this adventure for the rubbish left by tourists and the tide? If he found nothing he still wouldn't sleep but at least he would have had the thrill of defying the local constabulary and his parents who, no doubt, believed him to be fast asleep in his bed. He clambered up and over the dunes, the soft sand tumbling over his feet and into his shoes.

His heart-beat raced when he heard the approaching car. The lane was a dead end. The car had to be coming down to the beach. Instinctively, Mark switched off his torch and dived to the ground. He lay still, waiting, listening but not daring to look up.

Two car doors opened and slammed shut. "On the hour, every hour." It was a man's voice. "Make sure our bomb is tucked up in bed and undisturbed." His tone suggested irritability.

"Just enjoy the fresh air."

"No one'll come down here, Bert. Not with a bomb about. Even if they have made it safe. Not till they've checked the whole area, anyhow."

"Great. So we have a nice easy job. Don't complain. We could be breaking up fights outside the Tavern. Come on, a ten-minute stroll. Get some of that iodine down you."

Ten minutes! Mark didn't know if he could lie still and silent for ten minutes. He looked but could not see the policemen. He was hidden from them by a sand dune. Half way up the dune, his eye caught something that glinted slightly in the moonlight. He knew that if he made a sound he might be discovered but the temptation was too great. Impatience easily outweighed the risk. Slowly, using his forearms and knees, he edged forwards. As he tackled the slope, small cascades of sand pushed up between his fingers and fell over his hands. Somehow it felt reassuring, noise-deadening. He reached out for the silvery object. A camera! The moonlight had caught the reflector of the built-in flash. Mark's spine tingled with the excitement of the find and the danger. He could just make out the number of exposures. The meter showed the figure 20. How many were left? Four? Sixteen? It was the only way. Take the remainder and get it developed. That way, he'd find out if he had discovered something that his intuition told him there must be for every mystery: a clue. But he was getting carried away. His heart rate slowed as he realized that he probably grasped just another relic of the tourist trade – a lost camera. Maybe. Maybe not.

He nearly dropped the camera when suddenly he heard the voices again. Perilously close. He froze, his pulse drumming fast.

"Let's nip over here and back to the car."

"What's the hurry?"

Mark felt like crying out in agreement, "He's right. There's no hurry. Just walk round." He felt sure that the first policeman was suggesting a short cut over the dunes.

"You just love this peace and quiet, don't you?"

Bert laughed. "Maybe. But I just don't want to spend the rest of the shift with sand in my boots, thank you."

"Ah, well. You've got a point there. It's a devil when it gets in your socks."

Mark breathed a sigh of relief, particularly when he heard the policemen get into the car and drive back down the lane.

Stealth became Mark. He chose a tortuous, well hidden route back to the house. It was unnecessary.

For the whole time he had been out he had not seen anyone, not even the two policemen. He tiptoed up the stairs to his bedroom, clutching in his hand the night's trophy.

He lay in bed, watching the stars through the window. He never drew the curtains. His room overlooked the deserted beach and sea so no one could peer into his privacy. And the blankness of the sky helped him think. Unexploded bomb! It was too unoriginal. Even if the two policemen did believe that they were guarding one. Mark couldn't help but tie in the helicopters with Wednesday night's activities. If he was right then that couple must have found whatever the helicopters had been searching for since Monday. And, of course, if they had found something, maybe they had taken a photograph of it. Perhaps he wouldn't bother with the rest of the exposures but get the film developed right away. Or maybe he was just being fanciful.

The moonlight escapade had not only exhilarated but also exhausted him. Both tiredness and his imagining a quick end to the mystery contributed to his good night's sleep.

"Hi, Steven. How are you doing?"

Steven "Spielberg" Smith was one of those boys who was too rich, too spoiled, to be popular. His friends were always in need, yet it didn't seem to bother him. Looking faintly surprised at Mark on the doorstep, he replied, "All right. What can I do for you?"

"Well, since you asked, I've got this camera . . ."

"Call that a camera?"

"By your standards, no. But it does for me. I wondered if you could develop the film for me. In your darkroom."

"Er, sure," Steven said. "But why don't you just get it done normally?"

"Ah. I was hoping you wouldn't ask that. Some of the photos might be . . . confidential."

"Confidential?" A grin spread across Steven's face. "Oh, I see. You know Gene in year thirteen? She had some holiday snaps like that. She developed them herself here. Wouldn't even let me see them. Must have been a good holiday – some remote spot with her boyfriend, eh?"

Mark smiled. "Yes, well, I wouldn't be surprised with her. But I'm afraid I'm going to disappoint you. I don't think these are naughty like that."

"You don't know what you took?"

"I mean, no, they're not naughty. I . . ." Mark was struggling.

"Oh, it's all right," Steven said. "I'll do them for you. I can do it right now if you like. It doesn't worry me what you've been shooting."

"It'll just be between the two of us?"

"My God. They are important to you. Yes. You go for a stroll while I get cracking."

"I'd rather hang around."

Steven shrugged. "Take a seat."

The whole family was mad on photography. Steven's mother had quite a reputation in the locality and sold her work to the tourists in the craft shops in town. The spacious lounge that, in the distance, overlooked the sea was a gallery for the family's output. Photographs of old toothless fishermen mending nets. Old withered women selling the fish. Where did they dredge up these characters from another time? Mark sat on the sofa and waited for what seemed an age.

"Mark! You can come in now." The voice came from behind the door in the darkroom. "I think I've found what you're looking for." As he entered, Steven asked, "Are you in the Campaign for Animal Rights or something?"

"No. Why?"

"You tell me. You took them. Not too well. Look at the flash reflected from the wet sand. It is wet sand, isn't it?"

"Er . . . yes."

Mark was looking at two photographs clipped onto a string to dry. Both were close-ups of a dog. Its head was . . . Mark swallowed uncomfortably . . . eaten away. Most of it anyway. Not bitten like the dead fish that were washed up after being half-eaten by their predators. No, it was as if the flesh had somehow been washed away from the bone.

All the hair from around the haunches and back had gone and the skin that remained was tight on the bone, cracked and discoloured.

"Is it really that yellow colour?" Mark asked.

Steven shrugged. "It's difficult to say with a cheapo camera like this but I think so."

"I see."

"You do?"

"No, not really," Mark said. "I don't know what's going on."

"How did you come to take them?"

"You said that you wouldn't bother about the photos," Mark reminded him.

"Yes, well, we've all seen Gene – or something like her – and I've no desire to see her boyfriend at all, but this . . . I've never seen anything like this." Seeing the alarm on Mark's face, Steven put up his hand in concession. "It's all right. You can take them and I won't say a thing. I promised. Anyway, I don't think I want to be involved in anything like that."

Chapter 6

Sunday April 18th
I'd have liked a nice, safe, peaceful job making new drugs, oil substitutes or something. But all those jobs had gone. The dole or this. And now, if I resigned over a matter of principle, it would be pointless. That robot arm will be doing my job soon anyway.

Clearance wasn't a problem. I was never a student activist. My car was never spotted at peace rallies. Its registration isn't on their black list. I didn't join any political party either. On paper I look totally apolitical. Apathetic in fact. I did support causes, though – lots of them – but I never participated. So now I shouldn't feel hypocritical. But I do.

That's why I did what I did for CAR. But it failed miserably. Perhaps it's time I participated again.

My grandma used to start every conversation by saying, "It rained again today," or "It's going to rain soon." I used to hate her gloominess. It wouldn't worry me so much now.

Chapter 7

Last September, Sylvia had mixed feelings about leaving Crookland Bay for a new life at the university in Coventry. She knew that she would miss all sorts of things, from the sea, the sand, and the squawks of the gulls, to her family and friends. In particular, she regretted leaving Mark behind. But it turned out that life at university suited her very well. The freedom she enjoyed, the new friends, the social life, even the work. The chemistry was interesting, often challenging, and for the first time the teaching methods and the teachers themselves recognized that she was an adult. On her course, an early taste of industrial experience was deemed beneficial. Two terms at college to learn the basics, then six months out in industry. So, as

March rolled on, Sylvia had even more misgivings. This time, she had mixed feelings about leaving the university to return to Crookland Bay, where she was to work. She would have to leave behind all those new-found pleasures and tear herself away from the contentment of one special friendship that had developed. Still, the period at home would give her an opportunity to sort herself out, to think things through. In fact, one thing she would think about was whether that contentment was real. Maybe she was just making a fool of herself like some oversexed and overawed young girl. Anyway, with so many other uncertainties, she was pleased to get an industrial placement so close to her home. Physically, at least, she would be on familiar territory. She did foresee a problem, though. Mark. She knew that she couldn't confront him with her new relationship, certainly not until she was sure in her own mind that she had one at all.

The doubts she had harboured at first about the placement had been dispelled by her tutor before she left. She remembered how he had glanced at her ban-the-bomb badge before saying, "No, your principles can remain intact. The forensic labs happen to be on the same site as the MoD research station, but they have nothing to do with each other. Besides, do you think the military would let a sandwich student anywhere near anything . . . sensitive?"

"Put like that, no."

"It's a good placement, you know. You're lucky to get it. Or perhaps I should rephrase that. You were skilful enough to get it. They realized at interview what a good worker you'll be. Unless, of course, you simply used your feminine charms on them."

"That's right. The art of good interview technique is knowing how much leg to show."

He'd chuckled. "As successful as you'd be at that particular technique, you don't need it. Besides, I heard that you'd been interviewed by a female, Cheryl Judson – who is hardly likely to succumb to that sort of thing. Your other qualities must have won the day. But coming back to the point, forensic work's very interesting. It'll be good experience for you. You'll enjoy it too. Yes?"

"Yes, I hope so. I'm looking forward to it."

Dr Thorn had given a wry smile. Sylvia still wondered if it meant what she hoped it meant.

"Anyway, as you know," he'd continued with sincerity, "I've a lot of sympathy with your views. I wouldn't encourage any of my students to take up Ministry of Defence work. I'd refuse to do the placement visits for one thing."

"Thank you, Dr Thorn."

"We just have to remember that our views aren't the only ones in the university. You know this department has a high reputation for its research work and a lot of that is funded by the MoD. Without it, our reputation plummets and, like it or not, the value of our degrees will take a corresponding tumble. So we're both dependent on it to some extent."

"I suppose so," she'd replied. "But the work done here isn't really for the military, is it?"

"No. It's simply exploitation of spin-offs. It's not secret or dangerous. If it was, the MoD would keep it to itself. Anyway, Sylvia, much as I'd prefer to chat to you all day – and evening if it comes to that – I have this pile of practical scripts to mark and you know what students are like . . ."

"Awful."

"Quite. Always wanting their scripts marked on time. Some of them even expect me to turn up to give lectures. Like this afternoon, for example. But before you depart for those southern climes – say, tomorrow night – you'll have to let me buy you a drink. Then I can give you a proper briefing. Yes?"

"Yes. That'll be nice."

The department had made a good choice of Dr Thorn for student liaison officer. He was the youngest lecturer – only just out of university himself – and handsome with it. You could tell that he actually liked the students rather than just tolerated them. They all found him approachable. Sylvia was especially pleased to have him also as her personal tutor.

She started work at the forensic labs at the beginning of April. And, yes, he had been right. The job was fascinating. Samples varied from human skin and blood to exploding security devices for banks. There were lots of drugs for analysis too – street samples of illicit drugs and tablets for identification in overdose cases. She had feared that she would stand all day analysing for alcohol in the urine of drunken drivers but that was done automatically. No, she was set the task of developing a new method for identifying dyes in paint flakes. It was interesting even though she knew that the really juicy samples from murders, rapes and the latest drug crazes were only given to experienced staff.

Four things marred her first fortnight back at Crookland Bay, though. On her first morning at work, before she was allowed to set foot on the site, she had to pass through security. She was not surprised to be asked about nationality but some questions did worry her. "Are you holding a British passport? Are you a member of any political party or extremist group?" She answered all the questions but the security officer, on seeing the concern on her face, said, "It's all right, love. Just routine. I hardly need to tell you that some of the work on this site is secret, you know."

"Yes," she replied. "I know."

She was given a pass that identified her as an employee of the Forensic Laboratories and her attention was drawn to the instructions on the reverse side. They were just as off-putting as the officer's questions. "No cameras or any photographic equipment to be brought onto the premises. Go directly to your place of work and do not enter any other building. Do not pass any barriers displaying No Admittance signs. Do not touch or examine any equipment, machinery, instruments or documents without specific authority. After finishing work go directly to the exit gates; do not enter any other office, laboratory or building." She had never come across anything like that before. Life at the university was built on openness. Security, to Sylvia, meant something to hide and in turn that meant something underhand.

That same evening came the second problem. The one that she had foreseen. Mark called her. "Hi. Welcome back to the fold." Sylvia groaned inwardly. It was too soon. She needed more time. Anyway, she wondered, how had he found out so precisely when she was due back? Probably Mum – with her soft spot for Mark. "Hello," she replied. "How are things with you?"

"Oh, nothing much changes. How about you?"

"Yes, well, one or two things *have* changed for me. I'm fine, though. Enjoying it."

"Want to tell me all about it? Long time no date, as they say."

Sylvia hesitated. "I'm going to be busy, starting this new job."

"I know, but it's been so long. Besides, all being well, I'll be in the further education business next year. You can give me the lowdown on it."

She'd always had difficulty saying no to him, even when he came up with phoney reasons – she had given him the lowdown, as he called it, on a visit he'd made to the college in her first term there as well as in the Christmas vacation. But the last thing she wanted to do was to hurt him. "Okay, Mark, but let's call it a get-together, eh?" She put down the receiver and sighed. It wasn't that she had developed a disliking for her boyfriend, it was just that she wasn't sure any more. She recalled those times, not so long ago, when she could hardly wait to see him. That was when he seemed fun, adventurous, loving. Now it wasn't like that. She was away at university most of the time, mature, working hard. Mark was still at school – in year thirteen – still impetuous and still carefree. Sylvia felt that the love Mark professed for her was to him just another adventure, while she was now mixing with an altogether more sophisticated breed. And she preferred it.

Their meeting later that night was tense, unlike their easy exchanges of schooldays. She tried to keep the conversation factual – the new friends she'd made, the bands she'd been to see, the lectures and the lecturers, the marks she'd achieved in tests – but didn't manage to prevent its becoming emotional. It didn't help that she let slip that she'd been to a couple of concerts with Dr Thorn.

"So your *lowest* mark was 68%," commented Mark. "You must be doing very well."

Sylvia shrugged. "Not too bad so far."

"Better than I could manage."

"Don't do yourself down. You're clever – it's just keeping your concentration on work that's your problem."

"It's not my only problem."

"You poor thing. What else?"

"I've got a girlfriend who lives miles away and who goes off to gigs with her tutor. How old is he, anyway?"

"Thirty or so. What's that got to do with it?"

"I would have thought it was obvious."

"You can share an interest in a group and go to a club together without it meaning . . . anything more serious, you know."

"Can you?"

"Yes!"

"Well, you seem to have cooled off towards me. Remember, we're not on a date, we're on a get-together, whatever that is."

"Oh, Mark. Just give me a bit of time to re-adjust to life down here."

Afterwards, she told herself that, despite everything, she had enjoyed seeing him again. After all, he only needed to grow up a bit – to catch her up – then maybe . . . Maybe things could return to what they had been before she'd left school. But Mark's questioning *was* well-directed, even though she had denied it. Just what sort of relationship did she want to build with her tutor? She was not young enough and certainly not foolish enough to be merely infatuated with an older man. So if it wasn't infatuation, what was it? Really, she knew what she wanted it to be, but she'd have to watch her step. Why had he asked her to go to the gigs with him? What were *his* motives?

The gaunt young chemist who sat next to her in the canteen on her third day at work didn't make her feel any more comfortable. He looked at her over a forkful of shepherd's pie and said, "You're new here, aren't you?"

"Yes. I'm a sandwich student. Here for six months."

"Forensic?" When Sylvia nodded, he continued, "I didn't think they'd let students into our place." He smiled unpleasantly. Sylvia could not decide if he was being derogatory about students or the establishment. "Why? What do you do?" she asked.

"Tut, tut. You can't ask me that. Official secrets!"

That decided it. His bitterness wasn't aimed at students. "I'm sorry," she said. "I didn't mean what you do specifically. What generally? Where do you work?"

"No one knows. No one cares," he said, pushing his empty plate aside and taking hold of his glass of water. "I don't know why you bothered coming to a place like this."

Oh, thanks. That's real encouragement, Sylvia thought. "Actually, I find the forensic labs quite interesting. It's good experience for me at this stage."

He gulped his water down in one and stood up. "Let's hope you have a next stage." He went to walk away but turned back to her. "I'm sorry," he said. "It's been a bad day, research wise. I don't mean to put you off that nice forensic lab."

Sylvia was unable to gauge his true meaning from the mournful, almost pitiful face. She suspected that he was disguising his real feelings. For some reason he seemed to want to remain distant, enigmatic. He might be merely eccentric, he could be stark staring mad. She thought that defiance would do both of them good. "Don't worry," she said. "You won't."

The fourth event that unsettled her was a protest by the Campaign for Animal Rights. By then she had heard that the MoD research station carried out clinical research and for that they used animals but, being for medical purposes, it did not offend her. But it offended CAR, obviously. On this

Monday morning, a few hundred banner-waving protesters, probably including several of Sylvia's friends, gathered outside the main gates. She felt like a traitor caught red-handed in the enemy camp.

The site of the laboratories was beautiful, extending right to the cliff edge, as if to prevent an enemy attack from that side. The main block of the MoD research institute faced the sea so its workers, Sylvia supposed, had a spectacular view. She would never find out, of course. The forensic lab overlooked the main gate. No one even noticed that mundane view, at least, not till the day of the demonstration. Work in the forensic laboratory ground to a halt as the workers lined the windows to watch the commotion.

"Look. What a circus," said Cheryl, the laboratory supervisor.

"Yes," another of the lab staff replied. "All wearing their leather shoes and popping aspirins for the slightest pain. Protesting about animal experiments!"

"They're not all like that. Give them their due," Cheryl said. "Some really think we should test everything out on humans, prisoners preferably, rather than rabbits and dogs."

"The trouble is that rabbits and dogs are fluffy and nice. This bunch," he indicated the protesters, "only care about animals that look good. We could put slugs and spiders through agony and they wouldn't worry. That's why we all swat flies, and eat pigs and cows but not horses. It's a very selective campaign for animal rights. It excludes the ugly ones."

Sylvia did not wish to make herself unpopular after only a couple of weeks at work but she could not stay silent. "Come on. You can't generalize like that. I've a good deal of sympathy with them. I don't think animals should be used to test a new soap or whatever . . ."

Cheryl interrupted, saying, "There's the crux, Sylvia. The public at large – unlike this lot – accept animal experiments if it's for good medical work. It's just common sense."

"So," she asked, "it *is* clinical work that the MoD does?"

"That's the official line – clinical work, of a sort. We're not privy to that sort of knowledge."

Sylvia was about to ask another question but was prevented by the sudden high-pitched howling of a siren.

"My God," Cheryl exclaimed.

"What's happening?" Sylvia shouted as outside the building security officers suddenly swarmed like flies. A few, Sylvia thought, were armed.

"Fun and games." After the initial shock, Cheryl seemed to be treating it as a joke. "It means that they've broken in. Someone's breached the outer defences of our fine castle."

Other than the bustle of the security staff, Sylvia saw nothing to indicate the break-in. The sudden activity and the alarm that sounded had stunned the demonstration into silence. Then one of the protesters, realizing what had happened, let out a cheer. Almost immediately, that chant was taken up by the rest of the crowd and the wailing siren had met its match.

For the rest of the day, Sylvia kept her eye on the main gate but she never saw police arriving or anyone being led away. Strange.

It was eight days after the demonstration that Mark telephoned, wanting to see her again. His voice sounded different, anxious. "I tried to get you on Sunday – and last night," he said.

"Oh, Mum and I went out on Sunday, and last night I met up with some of the girls from school." As soon as she'd said it, Sylvia was annoyed with herself. Why did she feel that she had to account to Mark for her movements? Perhaps because he sounded so agitated.

"Never mind. I really must see you, though."

"Well, I can't tonight."

"Tomorrow, then, at the Tavern."

"What's the problem?" she asked.

"I want to show you something."

"Oh? What?"

"I can't say over the phone."

Chapter 8

Tuesday April 20th
My upper left arm is like a pin cushion. When I started this job, I had to undergo several courses of injections before they even let me near a lab. I was not really told what they were for. "They will offer you some protection from the toxic substances." That's all. And not much protection by all accounts. What we handle is lethal. If there were an antidote, we wouldn't be so interested. Usually vaccines are easy to make but this one is different. As far as I can gather, T42 has limited reproduction and its toxin is degraded slowly. A month, several months, a year. Then it would be safe to enter the release zone. Of course, us lowly staff don't have the complete picture. We just have our own little bits.

It's only Dr Richards who sees all the little bits and can put them together. It makes for good security.

There, I have taken an irreversible step. The mere mention of T42. Some new additive for petrol, or washing powder? Your whites will be whiter with T42. Increase your miles per gallon with T42. Hardly. Actually 10 ml of T42 would do for fifty square miles. Not immediately of course. We're not in the nuclear game now. We play it slow and sure. And subtle. It's because we're subtle and invisible that we don't draw the same publicity as the nuclear programme. Because the eyes of the world are focused on nuclear weapons, they are less dangerous. You should be looking at us. Here I am, waving as much as I dare, trying to get your attention and you just look the other way. Just what do I have to do to be noticed? You're too busy to answer right now but it's okay because I know the answer. Yes, I know.

Reading back over these notes, I see that I have used the royal "we". I wonder if that is classed as a Freudian slip. Sitting and loading samples for analysis seems so far from killing. Yet killing is what it's all about. By we, I mean the man who says, "Yes. Release it." I mean the biotechnologists and chemists like me, I mean the cleaners who sweep up the labs and offices.

I mean that I am guilty as hell.

Chapter 9

Sylvia always arrived early for appointments, even ones that she dreaded. Like going to the dentist. And now, seeing Mark. She waited in the lounge of the Tavern. It wasn't crowded. After all, it was Wednesday and only eight-fifteen. Even so, she could hear a commotion in the bar. She decided to buy herself a drink while she waited – at the same time she could peer through into the bar and see what the rumpus was about.

"Look," the barman was saying to a customer, "I can refuse to serve whoever I choose to. And you've had enough." The customer was hidden from Sylvia by the barman's considerable bulk.

"It's only eight o'clock or something." The customer's voice was slurred. Obviously he was drunk.

"It's got nothing to do with the time. I suggest you go home for an early night." A few locals laughed in the background. The barman moved to one side and Sylvia saw the drunk clearly. It was the morose MoD worker she had met in the canteen a while ago. He leaned over the bar and grabbed the landlord's sleeve. "Vodka and lime. Double," he demanded.

"I think you'd better let go and leave right now."

Sylvia dashed round and into the bar. She didn't know why she wanted to help him. It was hardly the allegiance of a work colleague. Maybe it was that pitiful look on his face. "It's all right," she said to the barman. "I'll get him home."

"You know him?"

"I don't know his name but he works where I work."

The landlord shrugged. "As long as he gets home. That's what he needs. Do you know where he lives?"

"No," Sylvia answered.

"Well, search his pockets for a driving licence. That'll give his name and address."

Sylvia did not like the idea of going through a stranger's pockets even for his own good. She took hold of his arm – the one he wasn't using to support himself against the bar. He only noticed her when he felt her against his arm. "Ah," he said, "the beautiful young recruit to forensic science.

Are they kicking you out too? You're not welcome here. Bad as the taxman. Forensic scientist in a pub! Collecting urine samples in the car park, eh?"

Sylvia ignored the questions. "What's your name?" she asked.

The man leaned his head on her shoulder and whispered in her ear. "It's an official secret."

"Well, where do you live?"

He tried to tap the side of his nose but missed. Staring in disbelief at his finger, he seemed to be expecting to see a hole in it. "That's a secret too." He stopped examining the finger and laughed aloud.

Sylvia looked at the barman, shrugged and started on his pockets. His driving licence was in the inside pocket of his jacket. Mr Paul B. Tedder, 15 Woodend Close. The landlord said, "Find his wallet, too. So he can pay the taxi fare. I'll phone for one."

"It's all right," Sylvia said. She didn't want to rummage around in his pockets any more. "I'll pay." She dragged him over to a seat while they waited.

"It's the highest form of killing, you know," Paul said.

"What is?" Sylvia asked, keeping her voice low so that Paul might follow suit.

"They say it's all the same as pulling someone's guts out on a bayonet. Same result. But is it any better – or worse?" He looked Sylvia in the eye. "You haven't the faintest, have you? Like all these people." He shouted to the whole room. "You haven't got the faintest. None of you. Not yet." He lowered his voice again, speaking just to Sylvia. "No need to declare war now. Just one man on a suicide mission. One vial. That's why it's worse." He hiccupped violently, then said, "I told them where to find the dog, you know."

"Dog? What dog?"

Paul got so near to Sylvia that she could feel his alcoholic breath on her cheek. "Spot!" He burst out laughing. He laughed till Sylvia thought he was either going to cry or be sick. It ended with another hiccup. A painful one, judging by his face. "No, it wasn't Spot. I can't say. It's another secret. But," he added quietly, "not for long. I've got the stuff. Tonight's the night."

It certainly is, Sylvia thought, especially if he's got more alcohol back at home. Tonight, his sorrows – whatever they are – are going to be well and truly drowned.

The door opened and a man's head peered in. "Someone order a taxi?"

"Yes," Sylvia replied. "Can you give me a hand?"

The taxi driver came in and glanced at his watch. "Eight-thirty! Quick off the mark, wasn't he, love?"

Together they walked him to the taxi. Sylvia gave

his address and paid the fare. "You'll be all right with him at his place?" she asked the driver.

"Sure," he said. "He's not as bad as he's making out. And it won't be the first time I've bundled a drunk into his home."

Sylvia had hardly got back to her drink in the lounge when Mark arrived. When her eye caught his, he was standing in the doorway, gazing at her.

"Hi, Sylv."

Sylvia cringed. After six months of being called Sylvia she had grown to dislike that abbreviation, a legacy and a reminder of schooldays. She resisted the impulse simply to kiss Mark's cheek and instead planted a quick kiss on his lips. She knew that he expected more but could not give it. "You look . . . good," he said, clearly unsure of himself after their last meeting. "Drink?"

"No. I'm all right." She pointed to her still half-full glass of lager. "I'll get you one. I've got more money coming in than you now."

Mark shrugged, obviously unhappy with the turn of the conversation and accepting the offer so they could get off the subject. "You look a bit rattled," he said.

Sylvia smiled and ran her hand through her dark hair that curled down as far as her shoulder. "And well I might. I just escorted a drunk from the premises into a taxi. I recognized him from work. Felt I ought to help."

Mark nodded. "See what riff-raff you mix with now." She smiled but his tone was tinged with sadness.

At least Sylvia had agreed to see him again. Even if it was only after appealing to her sense of loyalty rather than her affections. Mind you, why did he want to see her? Uppermost in his mind was her opinion as a scientist on the photographs of the dog. The fact that she was his girlfriend took second place – this time. But there would be other occasions.

She was sitting on her own in a corner of the lounge, looking as pretty as ever. If anything, prettier. Whatever Mark thought of her being away at university, it certainly agreed with her. There was an air of confidence, sophistication about her that was not there before. He was not sure if her contentedness charmed or annoyed him. He was in danger of being left behind by it, as if her move to university automatically qualified her for promotion to a different league. Perhaps it did. Having failed to achieve the "A" level grades he needed, he had missed out on a similar promotion. He was having to try again, to repeat the year. So now he found himself one year apart from her in education. As if that would make a difference, Mark thought, if she still loved me.

She took a long drink and sighed pleasurably as

she put the glass down, as if she had relieved a problem or great thirst. She saw him and smiled. Her greeting was a cold peck that once would not have satisfied either of them. They had agreed three years ago that, if one of them wanted to call it a day, there would be no holding back, no awkwardness, no apologies. A swift, clean parting. Back then it seemed impossible that they would ever put the pact into effect. For him, it still did seem impossible. He was less sure of Sylvia, though. Particularly after their first reunion. She'd seemed then to be holding back. Not to protect his feelings, Mark felt, but because she seemed almost ashamed of what she was doing. Of some other man, presumably. It was as if Sylvia was protecting *him*, unless, of course, she had simply forgotten their pledge to each other.

She refused his offer of a drink, making a pointed remark about his being dependent still on his parents while she had more or less gained financial independence. Mark knew that she wasn't demeaning him on purpose but all the same he cursed the year that separated them. He tried to make a joke out of her higher status but it only accentuated the separation. At first, Mark had regarded the year as an insignificant crack between them but now it was threatening to become a gulf. Maybe, Mark thought, events can prevent the gap from broadening. Maybe they can fill it in altogether. He badly needed that gap to be healed. He needed her.

"There's something I want to show you," Mark said, lowering his voice and looking around the lounge suspiciously.

Sylvia's brows rose. "So you said. Sounds interesting."

"No," Mark said. "This is serious. I really want to know what you make of these." He handed over the photographs.

It took Sylvia a few seconds to recognize what she was looking at. "A dog?" she asked. "What's happened to the poor thing? It looks revolting."

"What do you think's happened to it?"

She looked up at Mark's face. "How should I know?"

"You've done biology. Have you seen anything like this before?"

"No. But you need someone medical on that. I'm a chemist. Or trying to be."

"So you can't help at all?" A little of his frustration crept into his tone. He had banked on Sylvia's help.

"I don't see how I can, Mark. I wish I could. It's so horrible. Where did you take them?"

Mark had no real choice but to confide in her. Anyway, he had to tell someone. He couldn't have kept it bottled up inside himself much longer. The whole story came flooding out. The moonlight revellers on the beach, the camera, the developing of the photographs. "I didn't want to send the film away in case someone saw anything important. It's just as well with the dog in this condition . . . What's wrong, Sylv?"

Sylvia had stopped listening. Her wide eyes told Mark that she had been struck by a sudden thought. "It might be nothing. But that . . . Paul Tedder, the drunk who got chucked out, he said something about a dog. He said, 'I told them about the dog.' That's all. He wouldn't explain."

"'I told them about the dog.' Who's them?"

"I don't know. Do you think it's relevant?"

"It's a bit of a coincidence otherwise. Yes, I think it's relevant. I think it's the same dog." Mark, for days having dawdled impatiently in first gear, suddenly changed into top. "Didn't you say that this chap, Tedder, worked with you?"

"Not quite. He works on the same site – at Crookland Bay Research Station."

"You mean the Ministry of Defence place?"

"Yes."

"I bet they're mixed up in all this. Somehow. Come on. We've got to go and see your drunk. Where does he live?"

"But it's no good. He'll be out cold by now."

"You never know. Besides, I'll need you to introduce me. You'll be working tomorrow – and so will he, no doubt – so I wouldn't be able to see him till the evening. Come on, Sylv. It *is* important."

Reluctantly Sylvia agreed and together they walked the two miles to Paul Tedder's house. The night air was cold. Both Sylvia and Mark shivered, though for Mark it was more of a tingle. At last, he thought, something's happening.

It was an old house, the middle one of three in a terrace at the end of a short cul-de-sac. The boom of the big brass knocker echoed loudly. Sylvia imagined that, behind her, curious eyes would be peering round twitching curtains. She didn't turn to see if it was true. An unaccountable sense of guilt stopped her.

Mark knocked again. Still no answer. He took hold of the door handle and moved it down. The door began to slide open.

"No, don't, Mark," Sylvia said.

"Why not? We're here now."

Sylvia realized beyond doubt that she had out-grown his schoolboy appetite for excitement. But she followed him into the house anyway. Intruding on Paul Tedder's privacy seemed a lesser evil than loitering outside for the neighbours' entertainment. The front room was dingy, the windows being too small to admit much of the light from the street lamp outside. The room was also extremely tidy, reminding Sylvia of her own room when every-thing was packed away neatly before going away to university.

Mark whispered to her, "What was his name again?"

"Tedder. Paul Tedder."

Mark nodded, then called out, "Paul? Are you here?"

There was no reply.

"I don't like it," Sylvia said. "Let's go."

"It's all right." Mark had really come alive in this atmosphere. "You said he'd be out cold. Perhaps we can wake him. Come on. He'll be in his bedroom."

The kitchen was much the same as the lounge. No pans out on the stove. No towels dangling on the rack. Spotless, sterile. The stairs led up from the kitchen. They were steep and creaked loudly as they climbed, Sylvia behind Mark. There was no real landing. Three doors led off directly from the top of the stairs. The first door on the right was for the bathroom, the second the spare bedroom. That room too was tidy, with cardboard boxes stacked along one wall. Perhaps Tedder meant to leave the house altogether, perhaps he was moving soon. Sylvia was thinking these things so she didn't have to follow Mark into the last room. Let Mark find Paul first. Besides, he might be undressed or something. Then Mark's voice called through, "Sylv. You'd better come in."

The bedroom was even darker than the other rooms. The curtains were drawn, letting in only a faint glow from the street light. Ah, Sylvia thought, he's asleep. That's all. But he wasn't in bed. He was sitting on the floor, propped against the bed. Sylvia grinned with relief. "Couldn't even reach the bed, eh?"

But Mark wasn't smiling. The boyish excitement in his face had been replaced with something altogether more adult, more serious. "He's not asleep, Sylvia."

Suddenly the tension returned with a vengeance. "How do you mean?"

"He's dead. He's committed suicide."

"What? But . . ." It was so easy to imagine that he was simply asleep. Or maybe passed out. There was an almost empty bottle next to him on the carpet. His head had fallen forward onto his chest. He looked so peaceful. "Are you sure? How can you tell?" Sylvia had never seen a dead body before.

"Touch his hand. You'll know then."

"No!" Sylvia recoiled.

"Besides, look at this."

Sylvia was grateful for an excuse to look away, to tear her eyes from the man who earlier had put his head on her shoulder, his arm around her waist, and joked drunkenly.

Mark was standing by a desk in the corner of the room. Sylvia went over and joined him. There was a sealed vial standing on a couple of handwritten pages. Mark's hand shook a little as he moved the vial to one side and lifted the paper. Sylvia found herself wrapping her arms around Mark as together they peered in the gloom to read the note.

Chapter 10

*W*ednesday April 21st

Suicide Note
by
Paul B. Tedder, B.Sc.

Courage is not my strong point. I intend to improve my quota with alcohol. A few cans of lager are helping me to write this note. A few shorts in the Tavern will see me through the rest of the evening's business. Besides, alcohol will increase the effect of the concoction that I have prepared for myself. It is ironic that the forensic labs I walk past every dreary day will receive the remainder for analysis. I could report the mixture in this note but, look at it this way, by not letting on what I have used I will do my bit to keep in employment one forensic scientist. For what it's worth. Anyway, it will not be a difficult analysis – I will leave enough for mass spectrometry.

I considered using T42. My little protest would be more effective that way. Rest assured, the concoction does not contain it. I choose to make my point in another way. You see, I do not wish to harm anyone else and if I did use T42 – just think what would have happened when some poor person came in and found my body. Poor person! Poor country more like it.

This note is nothing like I wanted it to be. I intended to write a sane scientific report here – on my life and my chosen death. But the emotion, of which I know so little, keeps spilling out.

Actually, if you haven't already realized it, this is my second protest. Last Monday those two CAR supporters found the carcass room quickly, didn't they? And there's only a few minutes before the animals' bodies are incinerated, but they just happened to turn up in time to grab a dog used to test the efficiency of T42, our new chemical weapon. You know that they must have had some inside information. I admit it. But what good did it do? They bungled the job and the story that reached the press was . . . how shall I put it . . . cosmetic? Imaginative?

Talking of imagination, to help you imagine the appalling consequences if I did use T42, I will leave proof that it would have been possible for me to do it. I will place on this note a vial. The analytical section will soon determine that its contents are authentic T42. But you'll know even before finding this note that some has gone astray. Every drop is accounted for and logged. Until I took this batch today, the books had always balanced. Tomorrow, though, they won't. So you see, security is not as good as you think. Release of this charming, genetically engineered bug that synthesises toxins could happen – by accident or design. We don't have to wait for chemical warfare to occur.

There we are. My protest. My last report. It feels funny. I think I'll go to the pub now.

P.S. Don't drop the vial.

P.P.S. It's going to rain soon.

Sylvia could feel the lager rising from her churning stomach. She kept it down by swallowing again and again. Her conscience was making stabs at her gut as fierce as Paul Tedder's bayonet.

Mark broke through the silence. "Look, there's a sort of diary too." He flicked through its pages and then read aloud. "Listen. 'I wonder how it happens. A sudden impulse? A well thought out plan, painstakingly executed? It all seems too important a step to be decided on a whim, but could I sustain the courage for longer than a split-second? I doubt it.' But he did, after the drink." Sylvia could see in Mark's face the wild excitement returning, pushing aside the shock. "There's more. Hell. Listen to this. 'What we handle is lethal. If there were an antidote, they wouldn't be interested . . . 10 ml of T42 would do for fifty square miles. Not immediately of course. We're not in the nuclear game now. We play it slow and sure.'" His eyes scanned down the page. As if trying to pick out the juicy bits, Sylvia thought. "'Here I am, waving as much as I can, trying to get your attention and you just look the other way. Just what do I have to do to be noticed? You're too busy to answer right now but it's okay because I know the answer. Yes, I know.' Wow, this is hot stuff."

Sylvia sobbed to herself. In an effort not to show her weakness, she turned to anger. "Hot stuff! Is that all you can say?"

"What do you want me to say?"

"He's dead. Paul Tedder's dead and you think it's hot stuff!"

"All right, Sylv. Calm down."

"Calm down? Don't be so bloody patronizing, Mark, I don't want your 'There, there, little girl!' routine."

"I can't bring him back, Sylv."

"Don't keep calling me Sylv."

"What?"

"Nothing. I mean . . ." In her annoyance, she hit out at anything. She wanted to shout it but in Paul Tedder's bedroom it came out as an angry whisper. "Look," she indicated his body. "He's dead. Don't revel in it."

"Revel?"

"It isn't a show he put on for you. It's . . . sacrosanct."

"How do you mean?"

"Just . . . have some respect. He's sacrificed himself to warn us all. See the vial?" Sylvia put out her hand to grasp it but thought better of it and simply pointed to the pale liquid that looked as harmless as water. "It holds 30 ml, I'd say. The note said 10 ml was enough to kill everything in a fifty mile radius or something."

"Fifty square miles actually."

"Oh, I beg your pardon. It'll be all right then, there'll be thousands less people in fifty square miles! And 30 ml will only get everyone within 150 square miles. It's not so bad after all."

Mark sighed. "Sylvia. I'm as much appalled as you. Don't be angry at me. I didn't invent it. It's you chemists that did it."

Sylvia glared and her mouth opened to snap back but she fell silent. Her arms dropped limply to her side and the grittiness left her face. The anger had not waned, it was simply turned in on herself. "Not all of us, Mark. Don't blame us all. Paul Tedder was one. He blamed himself but look what he's done to stop it."

"But this won't stop it, Sylv . . . Sylvia," Mark said.

"How do you mean?"

"Well, this won't get reported. It'll be covered up."

"But *we* know about it now."

"That's what worries me. Look what happened to the couple who found the dog's body on the beach. They were whisked away."

Sylvia hesitated. "You mean, we'll be whisked away as well? We don't even know what happened to those two. They might be living quite normally somewhere."

"I doubt it somehow. Not if that dog still carried this lethal stuff. T42. But," he said, "if they are out there somewhere and have an ounce of curiosity, they'll want their camera back. What would you do if you lost a camera?"

demonstration that she'd witnessed last Monday. It said that the two protesters who broke into the MoD site had intruded into a lab that was working on a highly infectious tropical disease. "When they touched and smashed contaminated slides being used for research, both demonstrators became infected and subsequently died. The Institute regretted the deaths but the consequences of illegal and dangerous actions by CAR members must be realized. The responsibility lay with the two protesters, not with the Institute." The report seemed reasonable enough at the time. Now a different picture was emerging. Aided by Paul Tedder's leaked information, apparently telling them where and when to go, the protesters had entered a carcass room, taken the dog's body and tried to make off with it. According to the suicide note, they had bungled the job. Since it finished up in the sea, Sylvia guessed that when they realized that they were surrounded by security staff they had run to the cliff edge and thrown it over. Like a message in a bottle, hoping that someone would find it and expose the whole business. It hadn't worked, even though the helicopter searches found nothing. But then last Wednesday night, the authorities caught up with the couple who did find the body. The message had fallen on deaf ears. But could she and Mark be any more receptive? No, it was definitely too dangerous. This T42 had killed two already, maybe four with the couple on the beach.

"We can't take it, Mark. They say there's always a suicide note. They'll be suspicious without one."

"But we'll leave the diary. It shows how depressed he was. They'll think the diary *is* the suicide note. It explains why he killed himself well enough."

"We still can't do it. I don't know anything about this T42. I wouldn't know how to handle it. Should it be refrigerated, under vacuum, kept dark, or what?"

"Well," Mark said, "it's a bug. Genetically engineered and synthesizing toxins. Whatever that means. Surely it means something to you."

Sylvia looked helpless. "Not a lot. It's bio-chemistry and that comes in the final year."

Mark grimaced. "All right. I give up. I don't know what use this course is to you. We'll just leave."

"Do nothing? What about Paul . . ."

"Look, I've conceded in not taking the T42 and suicide note, haven't I? You concede in leaving. Someone'll discover him tomorrow. We don't want to be involved. Especially you, working on the same site. It'd look very suspicious."

Sylvia remembered the false newspaper report on the two CAR members. "Okay. I can't stay in here any more, anyway. Let's go – and hope we're not seen."

"We'll try the back door."

It was a small back yard, not really a garden at all. On one of the high walls a kitten was prowling. It looked at Mark and Sylvia suspiciously, wondering whether to jump down to them. "No," Sylvia whispered at it. "Go away." Just what did T42 kill? Humans, yes. But what about cats, cows, birds, spiders? Dogs? Yes, it killed dogs.

The gate opened into an entry between two rows of terraces. It was quite dark now and only the back of the houses overlooked the alleyway. They could get away unseen. But Sylvia remembered the resonance of the knocker when they entered, and the feeling of peeping, prying eyes. Were they seen? She found Mark's hand holding hers comforting as they walked away.

"What do we do now?" she asked. "Wait, I suppose."

"That's right. We wait to see what story emerges – what sort of story it is – before deciding what to do. And we try to trace the owners of the camera, of course. Not that we will."

"Do you keep the local papers?"

"No. Do you?" Mark asked.

"Yes. Lots of them. God knows why. Anyway, we'd better go to my place to search through."

Mark groaned. "I think I've had enough for one night. How about tomorrow night? After you get back from work."

Was this really Mark speaking? Normally he

could not rest till he got to the bottom of a mystery. And since when was ten o'clock late for him? Perhaps, Sylvia pondered, I misjudged him as well. Maybe the episode has affected him more than I thought. She did not wish to embarrass him by questioning his attitude, not after everything else that had occurred. "You won't have to wait till I get back from work," she said. "I couldn't go to work tomorrow – it'd be too painful. And too close to the MoD research station."

Mark stopped walking and looked aghast at her. "But you must! It'd be too suspicious if you didn't turn up. Just remember that your work has nothing to do with it. And besides," he said, "you can keep your ear to the ground. In case you hear the odd rumour or so. No James Bond stuff." He smiled, trying to cheer her up. "You can leave that to me."

Sylvia nodded slowly. "Okay. It makes sense. It won't be easy though."

"I know."

He seemed more understanding now. Almost gallant. "I just wish I didn't have to be alone tonight," she said. "Discounting Mum, that is."

"Your mum might like me but not enough to let me spend the night with you. Much as I'd like to."

There was an implication in Mark's words that she had not intended to prompt. She wanted the comfort of company, that's all. Someone with whom she could talk things through. "No, I . . ." She decided against correcting Mark's impression. It would have been cruel to tell him that she didn't want him like that.

Mark slipped his arm around her waist. "Come on. I'll walk you home at least."

She did not shrug him off. She found the contact soothing after the ordeal in Paul Tedder's house. "Okay, but why don't we call in at the Anchor for a quick one on the way?"

"I'd rather not, Sylvia. I've had enough. Sorry."

Sylvia was surprised. He did not look as if he'd had enough but obviously his mind was made up.

The streets were peaceful, the town blissfully unaware of Paul Tedder and the danger into which he had plunged them all. But not for long. The authorities would arrive in the morning, alerted by the postman or milkman, and take him and the T42 away. Then what?

The kiss with which Mark left her was very different from the one that had started the evening. She welcomed it, and his embrace warmed her chilled body. At least the night was not all bad. And she had dissuaded Mark from acting on the ludicrously dangerous idea of taking the T42.

Mark's hand did not leave her shoulder till he was at arm's length. "Goodnight, love. See you tomorrow night. And try not to worry about it."

Chapter 12

Dr Richards pulled apart the slats of the blind and watched the two distant trawlers as he talked. "It's a nuisance, I'll give you that, but no more so than the CAR incident. Somewhat less, actually. And look what a fine job you did on that." Behind him, on the other side of the large pedestal desk, the Public Relations Officer sat with a pen and notepad in his hands. Almost continually, he used his knuckles to push his spectacles back onto the bridge of his nose.

"I'm sorry," Dr Richards continued, now pacing up and down on his side of the desk and casting penetrating glances at the PRO, "to ask you to conjure up another story for the press but we simply cannot go public at this point. Consider the delicate stage of the Geneva talks and our pledge to do anything possible to further the negotiations. Consider also our renunciation of chemical warfare and destruction of our stocks in 1956. If this current problem gets out, no one would accept that we *are* still adhering to the principle of not manufacturing chemical weapons. We have an obligation to the public to hush it up yet awhile. No, I think we say we're still working on that highly infectious and fatal disease you discovered, which proved to be the death of the CAR members. You can tie in Tedder's death with CAR, actually. Their interference in the Institute led to the infection of a loyal public servant. The government regrets any death, particularly Tedder's, but CAR must understand its responsibilities, etcetera, etcetera. That's simple enough. What really concerns me now is the missing T42."

"Tedder's place has been searched from top to bottom. He didn't have it."

Dr Richards stopped walking. "Yes. That surprises me." He sat down at his desk and peered closely at the PRO as if expecting to see an answer in his face. "Of course, I might be barking up the wrong tree. It may be nothing to do with Tedder. But despite there being no mention in Tedder's diary of his taking it, my intuition tells me otherwise. Anyway, I've instigated security searches on all staff leaving the premises, and put out a call for a 'dangerous drug' through police, radio and television. All vehicles leaving the area will be searched and Tedder's friends and acquaintances will not be able to go to the toilet without me knowing about it." He shrugged his shoulders. "I can only wait."

"What damage could be done by the missing amount?"

Dr Richards sucked in a deep breath before answering. "It would depend where it was released. If right here, much of it would end up in the sea and be degraded in time. If it were released in Birmingham, say, we could say goodbye to . . ." He spread his arms in uncertainty. "I don't know for sure. The Midlands certainly. London would probably escape it."

"I see."

"The Ministry has been alerted. The Minister has called for an immediate inquiry, of course. Locking the door after the horse has bolted. With this and the CAR break-in, I imagine that many of us will not emerge unscathed. The chief security officer has already offered his resignation." Dr Richards' eyebrows rose significantly as he added, "I wonder if he'll be the only scapegoat."

Chapter 13

She felt furtive, contaminated, guilty. Sylvia could not help glancing at her work colleagues to see if their accusing eyes were focused on her. But no, the day was quite ordinary except that she dropped one sample. That was not like her at all. It was the cold dark shadow of the MoD building that penetrated the laboratory, reminding her of night and death. One thing was for sure – she would not be given any samples from 15 Woodend Close. They would be far too important for a student to tackle.

It was on leaving for home that she noticed a difference. At the main gates, all employees were filtering through the security building rather than walking round it as usual. Cheryl, who was walking out with Sylvia, groaned, "Oh, no. They do this at least once a year. It's to remind us about security. Stop people taking confidential reports to complete at home. Don't worry, it's just a bag search, not a full frisk. Unless they spot any funny bumps and bulges about your person. Mind you, with a figure and looks like yours, some over-enthusiastic officer might try it on." She smiled. "It's all right. Just a joke." Actually, it was more than a bag search. Coats and pockets were checked as well. It made Sylvia feel all the more guilty. Surely it wasn't just coincidence that the searches followed last night's events. She sighed with relief as she passed through the security area. In his hurry, the officer who dealt with her hardly had time to look into her face and see her blushes.

"I'll get it, Mum. It'll be Mark."

"Mark? I thought you'd forgotten him."

Sylvia ignored her mum's comment as she strode to the front door.

"Hi." Mark leaned close and kissed her. Sylvia was taken aback. She had not forgotten last night and the comfort she derived from his attentions but she had since realized that a bond born of shared misery was no substitute for one of love. And anyway, she was not convinced that Mark did share her misery. He seemed to wallow in intrigue. Right now she could tell from his excited, almost wild expression that he was itching to tell her something. It would be more for himself than for Paul Tedder.

"Have you heard the news?" He had hardly got a foot inside the house before asking. His haste was almost indecent. She shook her head. "Well, it'll be on in . . ." he looked at his watch. "Ten minutes. Local radio."

"What is it?"

"I want you to hear it for yourself first. Then decide if I was right last night."

"Hello, Mark. We haven't seen you for a while." Sylvia's mum had always approved of Mark. He was clean and respectful. He did not dye his hair, wear make-up or sport earrings, and he was from a good family.

"That's true, Mrs Cooper. But Sylvia's been busy at her new job."

Go on, Sylvia thought, ingratiate yourself with her and she'll try and integrate you into the family. "Mark's here because he wants to look through back copies of the local rag for some information in an old advert. So we'll go into the backroom. Okay?"

"Of course." She smiled endearingly at Mark. "Help yourself."

"You'd better fetch your radio, Sylvia," he said when they were alone. "It'll be on soon."

Mark had been right. The cover-up was as neat

and tidy as Paul Tedder's house. No mention of his work on chemical weapons, his suicide note, the vial of T42. "This morning a local man was found dead in his house. It is thought that Paul Tedder of Woodend Close died of the same infectious disease that ten days ago killed two Campaign for Animal Rights members. The day before their deaths, the protesters had broken into the compound of Crookland Bay Research Station where Mr Tedder worked. We understand from a spokesman for the Research Station that a full investigation is expected to find that the two incidents *are* connected.

"The area around Woodend Close was evacuated and sealed off while Ministry of Defence scientists made quarantine checks but it is thought that there was never any danger to the public. Mr Tedder was twenty-five and unmarried.

"Yesterday an extremely dangerous drug was among some items stolen from a doctor's surgery. Police are very anxious to trace . . ." Mark turned off the radio hurriedly before the newsreader got far into the next story.

"See," Mark said, looking triumphantly at Sylvia. "Tedder's death is not going to come over as suicide. It's going to be blamed on CAR. You can see it coming. But," he added, "they made a mistake."

"Oh?"

"If there was an infectious disease, they wouldn't

evacuate the area, would they? That would just spread it. They would simply seal it off."

"Yes, I suppose so. They must have got everybody out while they removed the T42."

"Presumably, yes."

"So where does that leave us, knowing what we know?"

"It means we want to trace the camera owners even more now – since you stopped me bringing away the hard evidence."

Sylvia frowned at him. "Wisely so," she said. "Anyway, come on. The papers are in this cupboard. Where do we start?"

"The incident with the couple on the beach was a week last Wednesday, so let's start with Thursday's paper to be on the safe side."

It took only twenty minutes of scouring the small ads. Mark was amazed when he found it. Monday's paper, Lost and Found section. "Kodak camera lost in/around Crookland Bay, Wed/Thurs. Phone Mr Eves, 0203 477011."

"That's strange," Sylvia said.

"What is? Oh, yes. The STD code. It's the same as yours at college. Since you're familiar with it, you can phone."

"Aren't we rushing into this?"

"Yes. Do you know any other way?"

"Well," Sylvia said, "we could talk about it first. We could be getting into a lot of trouble with this telephone call. In effect, you've stolen this chap's camera and developed a film that's not yours."

Mark smiled. "We are in the thick of it, aren't we? The camera's small fry compared to the rest of it, though."

"True, but we don't know the first thing about the person on the other end of this number."

"So we phone to find out. I really don't know what this advert means either. Perhaps the people on the beach didn't touch the dog, or whatever you have to do to get infected. Anyway, it seems that they survived it. I'm not sure how. But I can't see much point in speculating when it's easy to find out for sure. If it gets hairy, you can always hang up. And you don't have to say who you are."

"All right. But why should I make the call? It's your idea."

"Maybe. But it's your phone."

Sylvia trembled a little as she dialled. The feeling of guilt had returned. "Hello, 477011."

"Is that Mr Eves?"

There was a silence for a second or two before the voice replied. "Yes." It was a questioning, cautious reply.

"I'm phoning from Crookland Bay about a camera. I believe you've lost one."

"That's right. Last week. You've found it, yes?"

"Yes."

"With the film still in it?"

"Er . . . Just a minute. I'll check for you." She put her hand over the mouthpiece and whispered to Mark. "He's asking if there's a film still in it."

"Better say yes," Mark replied. "We've got to entice him down here somehow. And we daren't let on about the photos over the phone – we don't know who he is."

"I don't know why you say 'we'. It's all me," Sylvia protested. "Yes," she said into the telephone. "There's a film in it."

"Good. You found it where?"

Sylvia's face crinkled as she listened to his voice. "On the beach outside Crookland Bay," she said.

"That makes sense. Near where they turned up an old bomb?"

There was something in this man's voice that worried Sylvia. The accent, the tone, the way in which he phrased questions. Especially the way that he asked questions. It was familiar. "That's right."

"I think I'd better drive down to collect it from you. Yes?"

That did it. She did know who it was. Surely. She recalled his tutorial sessions. "So you're saying that you'd derivatize before gas chromatography, yes?" It was that "yes" at the end. Unmistakable. Mr Eves? This was no Mr Eves. She put down the receiver. She couldn't confront him till she had time to think.

"Is that it?" Mark asked, obviously surprised at the abrupt ending. "What have you arranged?"

"Nothing," Sylvia mumbled. "Just let me be for a second."

"What's wrong?"

"Nothing." Sylvia knew that Mark was reading her face. Disguise had never been her strong point. "I think I recognized the voice. It's my tutor, Dr Thorn."

"Really? Are you sure?"

She nodded. "He sounds different on the phone but, yes, I'm sure."

"Amazing. Is he the type to frolic on beaches with the opposite sex?"

Sylvia had not thought of that. No. Surely not. She hoped not. "Just a minute," she said to Mark. "I can check if it's Derek." She dialled a different number. "Hello. I need to find out a Coventry number. Yes. Dr Thorn. Derek A Thorn," she said. Then, "Yes. It's 27 Elm Road." There were a few seconds of silence before she said, "Coventry, 477011. Thank you."

"Clever," Mark said. "Directory Enquiries."

Sylvia nodded. "Yes. It's Derek."

"Derek, eh? And you knew his address. On even more familiar terms than I imagined."

One moment Sylvia felt cold and pale. Now she felt hot and flushed, as if caught red-handed. "He's my personal tutor. He invited me to his place for a meal. Along with his other students. It was nice. We chatted together a lot."

"I see."

Just what did Mark see? She looked at him defiantly but she knew that she was blushing. "Look. It's the camera that interests you. Not my relationship with my tutor. So what do we do now?"

Thursday night and a daunting pile of exam scripts on his desk. One of the worst jobs of the lot, marking exams. The full extent of their lack of understanding was heaped right there in front of him. He reached for the uppermost script but the telephone's ringing released him.

"Hello, 477011," he said.

It was a girl's voice. "Is that Mr Eves?"

The question stunned him. Mr Eves was the name he'd used in the advert! The camera had been found! He cleared his voice with a little cough. It gave him time to gather his wits. "Yes?"

The girl had indeed found the camera. On the beach too. Exactly as he expected from Ellen's story. A lucky break at last. The film would tell him if Ellen really had found some disfigured, diseased dog as she had claimed on the telephone.

He said to the girl, "I'd better come down and collect it from you. Yes?"

Suddenly the line went dead. "Hello?" No, it

was no use. The connection had been broken. The telephone purred in his ear as if pleased to cut him off. "Damn," he said as he replaced the receiver. He felt that he had in his hand the key to his sister's fate, only to find that someone had changed the lock. But was it deliberate? A terrible thought struck him. What if the police had found the camera? And his advert? If they wanted to discover how much he really knew about it, might they not set up some young policewoman to test him by telephoning, claiming she had found the camera? No doubt they could trace his true identity through the phone number in the advert. Had he given the game away?

He was still sitting by the telephone when it rang again.

"Dr Thorn?" It was the same female voice, but now using his real name. This is it, Derek thought. Now she's going to reveal that she's a policewoman. "Yes," he replied.

"It's Sylvia here. Sylvia Cooper."

Sylvia! Yes, of course. He recognized her voice now he knew. They had never spoken on the telephone before but it was unmistakably Sylvia. "Sylvia? You phoned about the camera? How come?" His tone echoed both relief and puzzlement.

"Well, it's a long story but, yes, we found your camera. And when I phoned just now, I recognized your voice."

"We? You said 'We found the camera'."

"Oh, yes. It was Mark actually. A . . . friend of mine."

"I see. You've got it with you now, the camera?"

"Well, Mark's got it actually. He's here with me. But we've got a confession to make. We . . . er . . . we developed the film out of curiosity. You see," Sylvia continued rapidly, obviously wanting to explain herself before being interrupted, "Mark saw you on the beach that night and thought there was something funny going on when those people came and whisked you and the woman away. He thought that the camera might throw some light on it. He thought that you were in danger, you see."

"Sylvia, what you've just said is very important and raises a whole series of questions. Perhaps the telephone isn't the best place for you to answer them, though. But I must ask if the photos do shed any light on what happened on the beach."

"Don't you know yourself?"

"No. Did they come out? What do they show?"

"There's two photographs of a dead dog. Horrible it is. But we know what's going on. It's not what the papers say. It was a chemical weapon."

What? Was she hysterical? No, not Sylvia. She was far too sensible for that. She must have really discovered something. One thing was certain – they could not discuss it further over the telephone.

Sylvia's voice was sounding anxiously in his ear, "Hello? Derek?"

"Yes, I'm here."

"Now we've found that you're OK, we're just puzzled how you escaped it. It's dreadful stuff. We've got all the details of it."

"Okay, Sylvia. I don't think we ought to talk about it now by telephone. But I must tell you that it wasn't me on the beach. The woman was my sister. The man, my brother-in-law. The official story is that their car went over a cliff and killed them both outright. Check it in your newspapers."

"No, I don't need to. I remember the accident. I'm sorry. We didn't connect it with the Tedder business."

"Tedder?"

"Well, that's something else you won't want to discuss now."

"Oh, right. Look, I'd better come down. I can get away . . . let's see . . . after lunch tomorrow. Give me your home address and I can be with you about five, I guess. Straight after you've finished work."

He took a note of her address and rough directions. "I'll stop over tomorrow night and Saturday too if necessary. There'll be bed and breakfast places still vacant, won't there?"

"Yes," said Sylvia. "It's hardly high season here. But . . . er . . . we've got a spare room. You could stay with us."

Derek couldn't help but smile a little. "No, Sylvia. Thanks, but bed and breakfast will be fine."

"All right. I'll see you tomorrow, then."

"Yes. Oh, Sylvia," he added. "Will this Mark be around to talk to as well?"

"I should think so. I'm sure he wants to talk to you, too."

"Good. Thanks. Bye."

Sylvia. Of all people, Sylvia was the one he would most like to leave out of this business. Sylvia and Ellen. It was already too late for Ellen. He hoped it wasn't too late to prevent something similar happening to Sylvia.

There weren't many female students on the chemistry course, so those that were stood out. Especially if they looked like Sylvia. When Derek first found that she was his personal tutee, he dreaded it. His only other glamorous student had been the soppiest of her year. She always expected her beauty to make up for what she lacked in brain-power. Amongst the staff she had acquired the nickname of "Worth-a-try". With a flutter of her eyelashes, she would ask for an extension of a deadline for coursework or a hint of what might crop up on a coming examination. When it was denied her she would say, "Oh well. Worth a try." But Sylvia turned out to be very different. She didn't thrust her beauty upon either her fellow students or the staff. And she was bright with it.

Derek remembered his first real encounter with her in class. It was at the end of a lecture. "And that, you'll be sorry to hear," he'd said to the whole group, "brings to an end this lecture course on chromatography. But we have ten minutes so fire away with any questions." Other than murmuring and the rustling of papers being thrust into bags, there had been silence. "Okay, no questions. Surely it couldn't be that the lure of the coffee machine is greater than the attraction of chromatography? No, it must be that everything I've said is perfectly clear. I'll expect 100% minimum on my exam question. No excuses. Go on, then, off with you, rabble."

He had been collecting together his notes when Sylvia came up to him. Unlike most of the others, he knew her even then because she was his own student. "Yes, Sylvia?"

"Just a couple of points."

"Yes?"

"A silly question first. Why's the separation of mixtures called chromatography? Chromatography means colour, surely. Chromatics and all that."

Derek remembered smiling. "I've never been asked that before. It's not silly, it's very astute. You're right. Chromatography's a misnomer, but an understandable one. The first separations were of plant pigments. These were separated into their various coloured components. Naturally the separative process was equated with the most striking aspect, the components' different colours. Hence chromatography – from the Greek for colour."

"That makes sense."

"You said two points."

"Yes," she'd answered. "About that experiment in chromatography last week. My results didn't seem to fit something you just said in the lecture."

"Really? Sounds interesting. Tell me all." She had gone on to describe a complicated effect which Derek always left to the more advanced course he gave in the third year. "Tell you what, Sylvia," he'd replied, "can I put you off this till another lecture? I hate to do that but I'll be covering it later when you have a bit more background on this and that."

Most would have been happy at that and joined the queue at the coffee machine, but not Sylvia. "Oh, come on," she'd said. "A bit of complexity won't hurt me. I can take it like a man, as you might say. Besides, I think I can guess some of it myself."

Derek had been taken aback and delighted by her attitude and initiative – rather rare amongst her peers. "Good. Let's talk, then. You having a coffee? Okay, we can chat about it over a drink." Her guess, as she'd called it, was quite accurate and her enthusiasm had stimulated him. Something it continued to do throughout the term whenever he had charge of her class.

She'd impressed too, in a different way, at their first social meeting outside the university. It was an evening last November when he'd invited all his personal students to his house for a mixer. Without Sylvia the evening would have died. They were overawed and largely silent except for Sylvia. She sparkled. He'd not attempted a full-blown meal but had prepared a high tea. "I'm afraid the cake's something of a disaster," he had admitted.

"I thought cooking was just like chemistry – mixing ingredients and heating for a bit," Sylvia had replied. "This cake's a great blow to my confidence in the staff."

Derek always enjoyed irreverent humour. It broke down the unnecessary barriers between staff and students. "You're right, Sylvia. You'd better not spread it around the rest of the students – or the staff."

"I wouldn't spread a cake like that around anywhere." She'd blushed a little after she'd said it. "No. I shouldn't say that. My cakes always taste like the back seat of a bus. Same texture as well."

When Sylvia was being mischievous, she reminded him of Ellen. And, like Ellen, she was very attractive. Her clear pale skin contrasted with her dark hair and eyes. If she had not been smiling and laughing so much, she would have had a rather sombre face. When he caught her natural expression, he noticed how her lips, prominent but not thick, turned down towards the corners of her squarish chin. The overall impression she'd made on him was immediate and favourable.

When the other students did open up somewhat, they seemed to think it was mandatory to talk chemistry and careers. "The course is biased towards industrial aspects these days," Derek had added to the conversation. "The Government only looks kindly on lucrative chemistry."

While the lads were nodding their approval, Sylvia had argued, "Yes, but we're here for an education – an experience if you like – not just training for a job. Not just fodder for industry."

"True. But you try telling the Government the difference between education and training. It'll be the death of real education, eventually."

"Oh, it's not that bad," Sylvia rejoined. "Things will work out all right. They always do."

Derek remembered just smiling in reply. He wasn't so optimistic as Sylvia but had no wish to bring her down. He applauded her attitude – and wished that he could share it. Even more did he wish that he could share it now that she was involved in whatever had scared Ellen so much. That's something else, he thought as he returned to the pile of exam papers, she now has in common with Ellen: insecurity. Her confidence was sky high at college, but today he'd detected in her tone an uncertainty reminiscent of Ellen. He shook his head and told himself not to compare them.

Ellen's death and now Sylvia's involvement made him question his relationship with his student for the first time. Before, he'd never felt the need to analyse it. He'd just accepted it as natural. They'd been out together for drinks, even a meal and a couple of concerts. Sure, it was unusual and closer than normal friendships with students, but there was nothing improper about it. He simply enjoyed her company. And he believed that she liked to be with him. On the occasion of one particularly enjoyable gig, they'd held hands and he remembered kissing her goodnight but it was all very casual and innocent. He assumed it was the same for her. Now, though, with Sylvia seeming to be as vulnerable as Ellen had been, he realized just how much he cared for her. They were hardly irrevocably entangled but suddenly it dawned on him that he'd grown dangerously fond of Sylvia.

Chapter 14

He loathed the telephone. Especially for difficult conversations requiring a degree of tact. On the telephone, Dr Richards felt crippled. He was deprived of the caller's facial expressions and gestures, that were so fluent, so revealing when words alone were ambiguous or even deceptive. Of course, he could exploit the situation too, but he'd never had trouble in disguising his manner as well as his words so he could always take advantage of the face-to-face exchange. He hated blindfolded conversations. In agitation he tapped his pen against a folder on his desk as he spoke.

"Our work here is often misunderstood. It is purely defensive in nature. To develop adequate defence – that is, vaccinations – against agents likely to be used against *us*, we – NATO to be precise – must have supplies of those agents. Therefore, we have to prepare them ourselves. But we carry out our research for defensive work, not to provide an offensive capability."

Dr Richards knew what the reply would be, so he had his answer ready. "Yes, but it was in the course of our preparations of potential chemical and biological weapons that we came across T42. We did not produce it as a weapon. We feared that others might develop something like it for offensive purposes, hence we were forced into the area so as to study the properties of such agents – necessary if we are to defend against them. We now know how difficult defence is in this case. But there's no doubt in my mind. Now that we have T42, we can and should maintain our lead in chemical and biological warfare – we call it CBW by the way. It is our superiority in the CBW field that prevents instigation of chemical warfare."

The tappings increased in frequency and volume as the young civil servant made his response. "No," Dr Richards said, "our work does not contradict the Government's promise to cease development of chemical weapons and destroy all stocks. We did destroy our stocks. And I'm not talking about any big re-armament, just keeping up the momentum that T42 has given us. In any event, we only carry out the fundamental research and some necessary initial testing. After that, the real testing, development, manufacture and stock-piling are effected elsewhere. When a friendly country takes those on board, there's no need for us to be involved in development or to hold large scale stocks." Dr Richards swung round in his chair to look out over the sea where the gulls cried raucously. "Of course there's a risk," he said. "After all, we are researching warfare."

He knew that he was talking to a new man at the MoD but Dr Richards had little patience. He could not understand why he had to justify himself to each and every ephemeral fool that the MoD employed. Actually, it was not a justification but an education for the novice. Successive ministers had amply justified the existence of the CBW unit but preferred the new generation of civil servants to learn the ropes straight from the Director of the unit. It was, of course, a waste of time. As soon as this new boy was acquainted with the full facts, he would be transferred to the Treasury or Department of Transport anyway.

"No. The 1925 Geneva Protocol did not ban either the manufacture or the stockpiling of chemical weapons. Also, whilst it forbade the use of chemical warfare, all nations that were party to the protocol reserved the right to retaliate in kind. Hence, NATO's need for continuing CBW research. Anyway, even under the present Geneva draft treaty, co-signatories would have ten years to destroy stocks and would be allowed to retain one tonne of super-lethal toxic chemicals for protective purposes." There. Justification well within international protocol.

Dr Richards put down the pen and occupied his itching hand with a paper-clip instead. "Yes," he continued. "As I said, I am convinced that we are well ahead of . . . anybody. But remember, we're not necessarily talking of a superpower threat here. CBW agents are cheap and easy enough for any tinpot dictator to produce. So all the superpowers are in the same boat for a change. The main threat comes in the form of state terrorism. Any state. Today, it's Iraq. Tomorrow, who knows?" He had a sudden impulse to invite the junior officer to the unit. Dr Richards would have enjoyed listening to his squirming excuses. But, there was just a chance that he was dealing with a budding adventurer rather than a coward, so he resisted the temptation in case the offer was accepted. "Exactly. The lead we take in the current Geneva talks stems from our strong negotiating position, the respect others feel for our known superiority. We must not lose that respect. The diplomacy lies in releasing information in controlled amounts. Just enough to reaffirm our lead and command that respect."

The civil servant was growing in confidence, querying the dangers of overstepping the mark. "I agree entirely," Dr Richards replied. "Nuances are the order of the day. Much more effective than hard facts and, unlike the latter, cannot be used against us at the Conference of Disarmament." He was not going to be drawn into discussing the value to an unfriendly nation of the news of the missing T42. He did not need to be made aware of the dangers by some raw Whitehall recruit. He brought the conversation to a close as soon as he could and threw into the bin the mangled paper-clip on which he had taken out his frustrations.

Chapter 15

Local MoD Worker Dies: Fears of Epidemic Quashed by Scientists

Yesterday morning a scientist from Crookland Bay Research Station was found dead at his home in Woodend Close, Crookland Bay. He had been infected by a deadly disease that the Ministry of Defence is studying. The same disease killed two men last week after they had broken into the Research Station during a CAR protest on the use of animals in medical research. Initial fears of a plague in the area were denied by MoD scientists following extensive checks in the vicinity of the dead man's house.

Paul Tedder, 25, was found dead in his bedroom by his landlady, Mrs Clara Robinson, who lives in the adjoining house. She said that Tedder was dedicated to his job and seemed to be interested in little else. "I set my watch by him leaving for work in the mornings. I was suspicious when he didn't show this morning." Later it was confirmed by an MoD doctor that the cause of death was the same fatal infection that last week killed Robert Noon and John Davis, the two Campaign for Animal Rights protesters who broke into the MoD owned Research Station.

The area around Tedder's house was quarantined yesterday morning while scientists carried out tests for further infection. According to the scientists there was no risk to the residents and the checks later confirmed that the area was safe. All restrictions on movement within Crookland Bay were removed early in the afternoon.

Sinister Link

The MoD has linked Tedder's death with the CAR members. Noon and Davis broke into the laboratory where Paul Tedder was working on the bacteria, according to an MoD spokesman. "Our laboratory practices and safety are first class, as was Paul Tedder's integrity as a chemist, but interference by the intruders caused an incident which we now know led to Tedder's infection." About the public concern and outcry for greater accountability of the Research Station, the spokesman said, "We contract out our facilities and expertise in many different areas, one being the investigation of infectious diseases like AIDS. Our laboratories are ideally suited to this important medical work, necessary if these fatal diseases are to be eradicated. I can assure the public that there is no danger at all, but accounting for the reckless actions of a few irresponsible extremists can be difficult. If there is a public outcry, it should be directed at CAR."

Anonymous Leak

Campaign for Animal Rights officer, Gregory Drake, repudiated the MoD view. "We regret deeply all three deaths. We must point out that none would have occurred if the MoD did not involve itself with dangerous work in which terrible injuries are needlessly inflicted on defenceless animals. Obviously there was an accident in the laboratories but there is no evidence whatsoever that it was connected in any way with Noon and Davis. We shall be seeking assurances that such an accident will not happen again and the only way is to abandon animal research altogether."

Drake revealed that Noon and Davis were acting on information given in an anonymous telephone call to CAR from an MoD employee disillusioned by the cruelty of the experiments carried out at Crookland Bay. CAR would not dissociate itself from the actions of Noon and Davis. "They were perhaps over-enthusiastic in their reaction to the information but that is condonable, given the sheer numbers and horror of the animal experiments involved. We deny that they contributed to the accident." Quizzed further about the telephone call, Drake admitted that he had no idea who had made it but it served to show that "all is not as harmonious – and safe – as the MoD would have us believe."

Paul Tedder lived alone and was unmarried. A full internal inquiry will be held at the earliest possible opportunity. The inquest on Noon and Davis is scheduled for 30th May. In the interests of national security, reporting restrictions will apply.

By the side of the report there was a photograph. "Paul Tedder: he died after laboratory break-in by CAR members."

Sadly, Sylvia put down the newspaper. Distorted,

she thought. They've distorted it all. Or what did Paul Tedder call it in his suicide note? Imaginative. Did she now wish that she and Mark had taken Paul's suicide note? What would they do with it anyway, against such a grand yet official conspiracy? The thought that Derek Thorn was on his way comforted her. He would be able to sort it out. He would tell them what to do.

"Sylvia," her mother said in her "I think it's time the two of us women had a serious talk" tone. "I know you like it up at university – which is good, I'm glad you've found your niche – but does it make being here at home so boring?"

Taken aback, Sylvia said, "How do you mean, Mum?"

Her mother put her sewing aside. "Well, ever since you've been back you've got grumpier by the day. And these last few days you've had a face like the back end of a bus."

"No, it's not that." Sylvia smiled. "I do like it at college but it's not better than being here, just different."

Sylvia found it hard to lie to her mother. In term-time, she was independent and with like-minded friends. Many years ago her mum had told her that schooldays would be the best days of her life. It wasn't true. Her mother had no way of knowing about higher education, the freedom and the opportunities it provided. Sylvia tried to find an excuse for her sullenness. "No, it's just that things haven't been going so well at work."

"It's no use me asking about your work. You've gone far beyond what I know about. But is that why this tutor's coming down to see you?"

"Yes. We have visits near the beginning and the end of our time in industry."

"Bit funny, coming to the house, though, isn't it? And on Friday night."

"We have to talk about my exam results too. There wouldn't be time for that at work." Sylvia wondered if it sounded as unconvincing as it felt to her.

"Anyway, you seem to be a bit chirpier now he's on his way." Sylvia didn't reply. She was not sure if her mother was trying to imply something or whether it was simply a statement of fact. "But what about Mark?" her mum went on. "What's happening with him?"

"Oh, Mum. Do we have to discuss it? I am old enough to sort things out for myself."

"I know you are," her mother replied. "But I'm not sure that what you sort out will be for the best."

"If I'm going to make mistakes, let me. That's how we learn, isn't it?"

"But some mistakes aren't easily remedied afterwards."

"Are we talking generally or about something

specific, Mum?" Sylvia said, the rancour clear in her tone. "I know how much you approve of Mark but I think he hasn't quite grown up yet. He cares for me all right – I don't doubt that – but for him a girlfriend is a status symbol. That's all."

"And you're above that all of a sudden?"

Sylvia could not bear the sarcasm in her mother's voice. "I'm going to wait outside. Get some fresh air." She stormed out of the room.

Outside she sat on the garden wall swinging her legs like a young idle schoolgirl. A cold wet wind was blowing in from the sea but Sylvia was glad to be out of the stuffy house, letting the breeze cool her, calm her down. And glad to be on her own again. She had always used the sea air for refreshment, and solitude was a tonic as long as it was voluntary and temporary.

When Derek Thorn's car came into view, she jumped off the wall and waved to guide him to the house. She almost ran to him when he got out of the car. "Hey, what's the matter?" he asked, placing a reassuring hand on her shoulder.

"Oh, I've just had a bust-up with Mum," she said. "On top of . . . everything else." They both looked towards the house and saw her mother's enquiring face turn rapidly away from the window.

"Am I your knight in shining armour?"

Sylvia smiled. "I hope so."

He squeezed her shoulders. "Well, you do have

a high opinion of me. I'll do my best but I can't promise."

"Look," Sylvia said, "rather than going inside now, why don't we walk along the beach and have a talk? We can head towards Mark's house. He'll be expecting us."

"Sounds fine," Derek replied. "I'd like to stretch my legs anyway. It's a long drive and I didn't stop for a break."

Sylvia looked at Derek and wondered why she found him so attractive. Sure, he was handsome but that wasn't all. When women go for older men, she thought, aren't they supposed to be after a father figure? Derek was nothing like her father, who had died some years ago. A burly man, he was. She remembered particularly his big, square stubbly chin. "Easy to hit," he used to say proudly. "Less easy to hurt." And his hands. When she was very young she thought he didn't have hands, only fists. No, Derek was not like that. Not rugged, simply fit rather than brawny. And Derek's hands were neither large nor rough, but caring. He was assertive yet considerate. Of course, he was intelligent as well. He would probably not remember the occasion, but Sylvia recalled with fondness the time she'd asked him some questions at the end of one of his lectures. No doubt to him her enquiries were old hat, boring even, but he hadn't shown it. He'd seemed keen and interested in their conversation, answering all her questions, posing others and leading her patiently through the difficulties of the subject. He'd bought her a coffee and talked as if he had all the time in the world for her. Not once, Sylvia remembered, had he glanced at his watch – unlike the other lecturers when you took up their time by asking them something. And unlike the others he hadn't made her feel small or ignorant. In fact then, and many times since, he did wonders for her confidence.

"What was this bust-up with your mum?" he asked.

"Oh, she was just nagging as usual." Sylvia felt that Derek was not yet ready to break into the subject of his sister, chemical warfare and photographs of the dog, so he wanted small talk. But was it small for her? Could she really tell him that he was the root of the matter? She could at least tell him half the story. "Since Dad died," she explained, "Mum's always been over-protective towards me. The argument was about Mark. He's an ex-boyfriend, you see. But Mum approved – strongly. So she's trying to get us back together again." Sylvia hesitated. If Derek did share her feelings, then this talk of Mark could upset him. She looked in his face but saw no sign of hurt. In fact, he smiled and asked, "But you don't want to get back together with him?"

Sylvia shook her head. "Not now." Should she

mention what was really bugging her mum? Why not? She was dealing with a mature man now. "But, it's only partly that. She suspects us, actually."

"Suspects us?" There was a hint of humour as well as surprise in his voice. "What of?"

Sylvia could not help but smile a little as well. "You know."

"But we haven't done anything wrong." He gave a wry smile and put up his hands, "Derek Thorn is innocent!"

"Yes, but not every student gets the same treatment from their tutor," she teased. "Do they?"

Derek glanced out to sea for a second then looked back at her. He shook his head slowly and sighed. "Oh Sylvia!" It was an admission that the inevitable was beginning to happen.

She felt comfortable in his embrace. It felt right. He kissed her, then said, "Come on. Let's get going before we give your mum – and the university – cause to complain, right here on the beach. Yes?"

"Okay."

As they walked, Derek's hand holding hers tightly, they watched the wind whipping up the waves. Reluctantly, Sylvia decided that the time was ripe to raise the issue that had really brought him to Crookland Bay. "What's with this Mr Eves, then?" she asked.

Self-mockery was clear in Derek's laugh.

"Embarrassing, wasn't it? When I was a lad, I was caught pinching some sweets from a shop. The owner shouted at me and I ran off. I felt much the same then as I did when you phoned for the second time. Caught like a naughty child. I don't rightly know why I used a pseudonym." He hesitated before saying, "Well, I do know really but maybe I was being too dramatic. I smelled a rat, as they say, and felt that the police could be in it up to their eyeballs. So I didn't want them to equate the advert, if they saw it, with me. That would have drawn attention to me. It suited me best to make them believe that I'd accepted the story they told me. For an occasion like this one now. Not having the police breathing down my neck. Maybe I should have had a showdown with them straight away. I don't know. Keeping quiet's a sign of weakness or prudence – I wonder which. Perhaps I was just drained after Ellen's death." Derek turned sadly to Sylvia. "What have we got ourselves into? Standing here like crooks, talking as if the police are the enemy."

"They are, Derek. We're sure of it."

"Okay. You'd better tell me all about it."

Sylvia was surprised how long it took to tell her story, particularly with interruptions from Derek. "But how do you know that these CAR members threw the dog over the cliff?"

"Well, we don't have any proof but . . ." She was

not annoyed by Derek's dispassionate probing of her account. After all, he was a trained scientist – he knew how to ask the right questions to come to unambiguous conclusions. She had expected her interpretation to come under his scrutiny, just as he assessed her other work – without regard for their friendship. After she had told him all that she knew, she asked, "What do you make of it?"

Derek hesitated before answering. "I think there's no doubt that a chemical weapon killed Ellen."

Sylvia expected him to say more, to decide what they should do next, but he was silent. It seemed to be his own private two-minute silence for his sister. She didn't want to interrupt his thoughts, and so waited for a while. "I'm sorry, Derek. You did once tell me – when we first met and you asked me where I came from – that you had a sister down in these parts. I only remembered after the phone call. But," she added, looking him square in the face, "I'm glad it wasn't you out there on the beach that night."

Derek continued walking. He did not reply to her comment. Instead, he said, "I was down here last Friday and Saturday actually."

Sylvia frowned. "Why didn't you call in on me?"

"I didn't want to drag you into this affair. Ironic, isn't it? Besides, I wouldn't have been good company. My mind was on Ellen. We were very . . ."

He struggled to find the right words. "She was a bit like you, really. I was very fond of her."

"Yes. I'm sorry."

Derek breathed deeply. "Come on," he said. "I think we'd better see Mark now. Let me hear his story and then we'll decide what to do. If we can."

By an unspoken mutual consent, their hands parted as they approached Mark's house. That, Sylvia thought, means that we both feel guilty.

Mark's parents were out so the three of them were able to talk it all over in his house. Sylvia was content to sit and watch as Mark, obviously impatient for action, narrated his version of events. The two men were totally unalike. Not only was Mark much younger, he was taller and thinner too, skinny even. His hair was short and blond, Derek's was longer and dark with a dash of grey here and there. Sylvia put an end to the comparison. It was too much like weighing up two blouses before deciding which to buy. They could be quite different yet each could have its attractions. But there again, maybe only one would fit.

"So you see," Mark concluded, "we have all the proof we need to expose them."

"Proof?" Derek queried.

Mark waved the photographs of the dog at Derek. "These for instance."

"What do they show, Mark?"

"Well, a dog. A dog that's been experimented on with a chemical weapon."

"Do they?" Derek replied. "Not a dog with a rare tropical disease? You must be careful. The photographs could be used to substantiate the claims of the authorities. They're not conclusive."

"What about the diary that explained the weapon? The genetic engineering, whatever that is."

"Can you produce the diary? No. I'm afraid you haven't got anything that proves we're not dealing with an infectious disease. The best you can do is to show that there was a cover-up over Ellen and Jack. But they'll explain that by saying that it was to allay public panic."

"Are you saying that we can't do anything?" Mark said, frustrated by Derek's sobriety.

"No, I'm not saying that, but you can't talk about exposing them. Remember that by producing chemical weapons they haven't done anything wrong – in the legal sense." Derek put up his hand to prevent the protests from both Mark and Sylvia. "Chemical warfare's in the science news a lot these days. Last night I took the opportunity to check out the facts. There's nothing to stop nations making and storing chemical weapons. A convention has only banned their use, not their manufacture."

"Why make them if you can never use them?"

"Retaliation in kind is allowed. In other words," Derek exlained, "if someone attacked us with a chemical weapon, we could legally retaliate with a chemical attack on them. Hence, one justifies having some chemical warfare capability. And of course, there's the balance of terror argument. Just like the nuclear situation. Made not to be used. As long as all countries have the weapons, no one dares use them – or so the argument goes. Weapons made not to be used actually keep the peace." Derek gave a wry smile. "It's a difficult argument to counteract. The fact is that peace has been maintained. But does that make the argument correct? No. Of course not. But one can only disprove it on the day that war breaks out – when it's too late."

There was a silence before Sylvia said, "Maybe legally it's okay but morally it must be wrong."

"I believe it is," Derek replied. "Very much so. But the fact remains that peace has been maintained, more or less, even with the proliferation of chemical and nuclear weapons. *Some* would say because of it. Since the war, chemical weapons have only been used against those unable to retaliate – as in Vietnam and Iran. That does add weight to the balance of terror argument. Surely you can see that it would be foolhardy of us to say that we are definitely right and they are definitely wrong."

Sylvia could see by his reddening face that Mark was getting more and more frustrated. "So we do nothing," Mark cried, "till a war does break out. Or an accident occurs, as Tedder pointed out in his notes. Then we say, 'Ah, we were right after all. Pity we didn't do anything about it.'"

"I haven't said that we should do nothing," Derek answered. "Just that we must be very careful with issues that aren't simple. Not black and white. For instance, right now there are talks going on in Geneva on chemical disarmament. We have to think about that too. How would you feel if we did anything rash and as a result killed off the talks?"

"Okay. Not very good. But at least I would have taken a stand. To stop something I know is wrong." Mark looked defiantly at Derek then said, "Remember your sister. Don't you care that this T42 killed her?"

Sylvia looked aghast at Mark. Should she rebuke him? Or should she fly to Derek's side, as she longed to do? She couldn't. Not without aggravating Mark. She watched Derek and waited. His face showed pain for a moment, then he turned directly but calmly to Mark and said, "Yes. I care. I know what she must have gone through. You see, from what you've said, I think I know what they're using. I know the symptoms. Vomiting and diarrhoea at first. Then there's trembling, skin irritation and dizziness. It ends with decomposition of the skin and haemorrhaging. That's how my sister will have died."

Mark made no reply.

Sylvia wanted to defuse the situation but knew that she could not change the subject altogether without seeming frivolous and uncaring. She appealed to Derek's rationality instead. "What is this weapon, then? It involves genetic engineering and a toxin."

"Yes." Derek seemed to be dragging himself back to reality. "Yes. You know that certain plants and animals produce poisons – like some spiders and poisonous snakes. There are also some particularly nasty poisons, called toxins, produced by moulds that grow on contaminated food. You could isolate those toxins for use as a weapon but how do you administer them?" Sylvia saw with relief that by taking on his favourite role of teacher, Derek was slowly pushing to the back of his mind his private grief. "It sounds, from what you've told me, that the MoD has developed an ingenious approach through genetic engineering."

"What's that?"

"You know about genes, yes? They control our characteristics. Production of all the chemicals that we're made of, is controlled by our genes. That's why I have blue eyes and Sylvia has that funny auburn tint in her hair. Unless it's dyed, of course."

He could even smile now. "Genes govern all life forms. So the production of toxins by moulds is controlled by a gene. It's possible to isolate that gene and transplant it into another living thing. I think they may have transplanted it into what was a harmless but very infectious bacterium. One that's hard to innoculate against, presumably. Such a bacterium could easily be used in warfare because it would spread like any other infectious bacteria. But it would also be producing toxin. Anyone infected would be poisoned by it. Diphtheria and malaria operate in the same sort of way. They invade the body then release their poisons into the bloodstream or wherever. The only difference is that they're not man-made."

"So when the research station says it's working on infectious diseases, it's not far out?" Sylvia asked.

"It's perfectly true. Only they made the bug in the first place."

"And when you said you saw some men spraying the beach. . . ?"

Derek nodded. "They were trying to decontaminate it, presumably. A disinfectant or antibiotic would kill the bug and stop it spreading. Then there's traces of the toxin to clear up. It would be degraded in time, probably by the action of sunlight."

"But you said it would be difficult to disinfect

this particular one and from Tedder's notes too it seems as if it's not easy to kill it off," Mark commented. "Otherwise they wouldn't be interested in it as a weapon, it said in his diary."

"No doubt that's true," Derek replied. "But it's not like in a war. On an uninhabited beach, they could use rather drastic agents to kill it. If it had been let loose in a city they wouldn't be able to use the strong stuff – the cure would be as fatal as the disease. Anyway, I don't think that you should worry, Mark, because you went on the beach. If there was still a risk they'd have to keep birds, crabs and fish away. Policemen too. I doubt if there was much left after the dog had been in the sea for a few days. Probably only fairly close contact with the dog itself would be fatal." He hesitated and drew a deep breath. "No, they must be convinced that they disinfected the beach – either because there wasn't much left or because they could use strong disinfectants."

"Oh, I'm not worried for myself," Mark replied.

No, Sylvia thought. You wouldn't be, being so reckless. She was glad she had persuaded him not to take the T42. Otherwise he'd be dreaming up all sorts of crazy, frightening schemes for it in an attempt to stop further manufacture.

Chapter 16

"It was the photograph in the paper. I recognized him straight away."

"I see. And you picked him up at what time, did you say?"

"Eight-thirty, at the Tavern. I was surprised, being drunk so early. I looked at my watch. Eight-thirty exactly, it was."

"Um. Was anyone with him in the pub?"

"Yes. A young girl. Good-looking. About . . . er . . . eighteen. Twenty at the outside."

"Just a girl? No one else?"

"That's right."

"I think you'd better see our resident artist."

"How do you mean?"

"I bet you've always wanted to see how we

produce those photofits for newspapers and posters – 'Have you seen this girl?' You're going to help to produce a likeness of her. Do you think you can do that?"

"I should think so. I've got a good memory for faces."

"Yes. I remember. He was drunk." The landlord felt a sudden chill. One minute ranting and raving for a drink, the next . . . Perhaps he should have served him after all. Maybe he wasn't drunk anyway. It could have been the effect of this disease that he'd read about in the paper.

"Now. Think carefully and have a look at this girl. Have you seen her at all?"

The barman looked at the picture and recognized her straight away. "Oh yes," he said, looking directly into the policeman's face to show his confidence. "She was the good Samaritan of the piece. She stopped him making a fool of himself over the drink and paid for the taxi home."

"So, you gather that she knew him?"

"Yes and no. Let me think. She said, 'I don't really know him but he works at the same place as me.' Or something like that."

"Really? You're sure about that?"

"Yes, definitely. She had to go through his pockets to find his name and address."

The policeman wrote a few notes on a pad then

asked, "Did they talk together before the taxi came?"

"I don't rightly know. I suppose so. They sat together. Oh. At one stage, the chap shouted something. What was it, now? 'You haven't got the faintest idea. Not yet.' Is that important?"

The policeman shrugged non-committally. "This girl, she was alone?"

"Yes. At least, at first. She was joined later by a young lad."

"Did you know him?"

"No. He's been in before, I think, but I wouldn't say I know him."

"I see. Can you describe him?"

"Well, I see a lot of faces in here. It's not easy, but I can give it a go."

Chapter 17

Teachers are actors. Derek had the reputation of being an exhibitionist lecturer. He would prowl around the lecture room, make jokes, stand on his head if he thought that it would help to get his message across. Students absorbed and remembered ideas better if they were entertained at the same time as being taught. But it was all an act. Derek wasn't really like that. He preferred the shadows, only taking the limelight when his job required it. Given the option, he would disappear into a crowd rather than address it on a soap-box. He wondered if Sylvia had fallen for Derek the exhibitionist or Derek the silent and not so strong. Did she even know that there were two Dereks? Sooner or later she would see the real thing. What would she think of him then?

Like any actor, he had mastered emotions. He could be seething inside yet outwardly calm. That was how he now felt as he talked with Mark and Sylvia. He could not get out of his mind a picture of Ellen, not as she used to be, but as a war victim. Bloody and disfigured. He wondered what they had done with her body. One thing was certain, they would not have put it in the car when they set fire to it and pushed it over the cliff. That might not have destroyed all traces. No doubt both she and Jack had died in some isolation ward in a hospital – a military hospital probably. Their bodies would have been incinerated, more efficiently than if they had been in the flaming car. Really, Derek wished he could wreak some drastic revenge as Mark would have done. But Mark did not see the wider issues. It was a while since Derek had exchanged his own youthful, straightforward sense of right and wrong for adult uncertainty and responsibility. He had been like Mark, though, till he outgrew arrogance and gained inhibitions. He wasn't sure whether the transition had made him a better person or simply an older one. In some ways he would like to be like Mark again.

He wondered how Mark regarded Sylvia. She'd described *him* as an ex-boyfriend, but did Mark think of Sylvia as an ex-girlfriend? He doubted it. Derek could envisage all too easily how a tug-of-war for Sylvia might develop. If it did, she could get hurt whatever the outcome. Derek would not expect Mark, with all his youthful competitiveness, to withdraw to prevent Sylvia's suffering. So it was up to Derek. She wouldn't get hurt if he exercised restraint and didn't get too involved with her. It seemed logical, with her mother, the university, their age gap and Mark all against them. But being logical didn't make self-control desirable – or easy. Given his new found affection for her, he would love to take an irrevocable step.

"Okay," Derek said to them, "I think I see how we should tackle this whole thing. I want to bypass the police because I'd be on unfamiliar territory. And I'm not sure just how much they know anyway. But there is a breed I do know all about – the chemists. I think I'll arrange a meeting with the head of the Research Station."

"Dr Richards," Mark put in. "It said so in Tedder's diary."

"Yes. Richards. The trouble is," Derek went on, "that if I go now, he'll want to know where I got all my information. It wouldn't be long before he got back to you two. So I need to have enough facts to put before him that could have been gained independently of the two of you. I'm thinking mainly about the events surrounding Ellen and Jack's 'accident'. Having seen men spraying the beach, one thing I'd like is a sample of the sand to take back to the university where I can analyse it."

"But," Sylvia objected, "you said that the T42 would be gone by now."

"True, but I'm after whatever they used to treat the beach. You don't defuse a wartime bomb by spraying it with disinfectants. If I find disinfectants, I've got hard facts to put before Richards. Of course, it won't rule out the infectious disease argument but for that I can turn elsewhere. To carry out genetic engineering, they'd need special chemicals and equipment that can hardly be used for anything else. I should be able to check if the research station has ordered such things."

"How?"

"I just happen to have an old university friend working at the major suppliers of those items."

"So what do we do right now?" Mark asked.

"Well, not a great deal. The only thing I need is that sample of sand. I'll get it from the beach tonight."

"There's police patrols," Mark warned. "But I've done it before. Why don't I do it again? I know the area better than you as well."

Derek shrugged. Why not let Mark vent his yearning for action on another moonlight escapade to the beach? It was less dangerous than other actions that he might be contemplating. "Okay. I suggest you wear some good wellies and rubber gloves. Afterwards, throw the gloves away and thoroughly wash the wellies. Just in case. I'll go back home tomorrow and I can do the analysis next week. Towards the end of the week I can organize an industrial training visit to you, Sylvia, and a meeting with Richards at the same time." Derek saw consent in both of their faces. He added, "You two mustn't do anything till I get back, okay?" He looked directly at Mark.

"Okay," Mark agreed.

Sylvia nodded.

There are two reasons, really. First, because he can't see that this chemical warfare must be stopped and, second, because of Sylv. They didn't sit together, didn't start petting on the couch or anything, but it was as plain as day that he's got something going with Sylv. It's Thorn that's driving a wedge between us. Mark wasn't sure how he knew, but he did. Maybe it was the way they positively avoided sitting together. Anyway, now she's got her mind set on him, she's forgotten how good it was between us on Wednesday – when we found Tedder. Yes, and she would have wanted more if I hadn't had other things on my mind. Now it's Derek this, Derek that. Her hero! But he isn't going to do anything worthwhile, this college chemist. That's why I hate him. For two reasons.

Oh, I'll wait till after his little chat with Richards but it won't come to anything. I can see that it'll be up to me. Just like it's up to me to get the sand tonight. What will those two be doing tonight while I'm out on the beach – trying to avoid the police and the chemicals? I don't need much imagination to guess.

It was getting quite dark as Sylvia and Derek walked back along the beach. For Sylvia, the shore and the rhythm of the sea had always promised romance but, knowing what they had done to Ellen, did they hold the same magic for Derek? As they strolled, Derek kept his distance. Not through a lack of interest, she now knew, but because something was holding him back. Perhaps the memory of Ellen and Jack on part of this very beach.

Restraint had never been a virtue of boys of her own age. She'd had to fight them off. They'd always been so impatient, so demanding, their clumsy groping ruining passion. Mark too, on their second date, almost three years ago now. Even if he had been able to undo her bra – the clasp was at the front, not the back where he searched – she would not have let him go further. Any excitement she'd felt in those days was not passion but the thrill of doing something considered wrong. She'd wanted it to be romantic, not sleazy. No, when the boys at school first became aware of sex, Sylvia and her friends had a term for the most impatient ones. It was silly, of course, but in those days the whole business was silly. They used to say, "Watch that Tommy Williams, he's got desert disease – wandering palms." Maybe it was due to boys like Tommy Williams that she remained a virgin for so long before succumbing to Mark's persistence. Of course, Mark outgrew clumsiness and it wasn't ever sordid exactly, yet for her it had never attained a tenderness that she felt love-making should have.

But Derek . . . He roused her without once fumbling inside her clothes. But fumbling wasn't the right word for Derek. She couldn't imagine him being anything but deft and affectionate. Unfortunately, Sylvia thought, imagination is all it is. He excited her without even trying. He was probably unaware of the feelings that he evoked in her just by the way he looked at her and by his simple, innocent touching of her arms and shoulders. It dissolved any resistance she might have had and she longed for him to make love to her.

"Look, Derek," she said, "I know you won't accept the offer of our spare room but why don't I come and see you settled into your boarding house?"

Derek smiled. "No. I'm not sure I could trust myself with you."

"I'm not a kid, Derek."

"But you are my student. Come on, we'll go back to your house. I'll collect my car and find my way from there to those bed and breakfast places. I will see you in the morning before I go back."

"What about a drink, or a meal maybe?"

"I'd love to, Sylvia, but let's restrict this meeting of ours to business-like hours. Save any more aggro with your mum."

"Who cares?" She paused and sighed. "I suppose I do." Besides, she knew that she wasn't going to change his mind by arguing further. "Okay. We'll go back. But," she looked at her watch, "it's only seven-thirty. There's no need to rush, is there?"

"None at all."

Hopes of an early summer, rife a couple of weeks back, had been dashed. Even so, as Derek and Sylvia dawdled along the beach, it wasn't too cold or blustery to be uncomfortable. Derek stopped to turn over with his foot a curious stone but found that the other side was oil-stained. "The chemical industry isn't doing this coastline any favours at all, is it?" he said.

Sylvia frowned. "No," she replied simply, sadly.

He sighed. Then, changing the mood, he asked, "What's Mark hoping to do after 'A' levels?"

"College or university if the grades are good enough this time."

"This time?"

"He's doing a repeat year," Sylvia said.

"Oh? So what went wrong last year?"

Sylvia winced and stopped walking. She didn't really want to go into it. She knew very well that she could not be blamed for Mark's failure but still she was at the heart of it – the root cause. "Let's just say that when he should have been revising he was . . . pestering me to go out with him as normal. But I wouldn't jeopardize my own exams. I said, 'It's only for a couple of months I want to concentrate on revising. You should too!' A few weeks apart wouldn't have hurt him, but . . . well . . . he turned moody. You know, 'If I can't see you I won't be able to revise anyway.' It was just a difference in emphasis. He wanted us to enjoy ourselves as usual, exams or no, and I needed to work more. He just blew the whole thing up really."

"You're not saying that he fluffed it on purpose, just to spite you, are you?"

"No," Sylvia said. "But I think he refused to revise to spite me. He's clever enough, you know. Cleverer than me. He thought he wouldn't need to revise to get the grades he wanted."

"I hope this current problem doesn't make him forget his exams again."

"I should hope not. He should have learned. You may not see it but he's very angry about last year."

"Angry with you?" Derek asked.

Sylvia hesitated. "No. Not with me. He's . . ." She looked at Derek and knew that she could be open with him. "You see, he loves me – so he can't be that angry with me. No, I'm sure he blames himself."

Derek nodded. "He could be very angry with me too now, of course."

"How do you mean?"

"He's angry with himself because it's his own fault he got left behind at school while you went off to university. He'll be angry with me for . . . associating with you there."

Sylvia looked at him. "What do you mean?" she asked.

"Now it's your turn to act innocent, eh?"

Like Derek earlier, she put up her hands. "You haven't made a dishonest woman of me."

Derek laughed. "No. But, as you said yourself, Mark's not stupid. He can see that the university's changed you, and he thinks there's more to you and me than tutor and student."

"Yes," she replied soberly. "I guess you're right." Then she looked at Derek with a cheeky grin and said, "Mark's right, too. Isn't he?"

"It's wonderfully peaceful by the sea at night." He smiled. "Don't you agree?"

Sylvia amazed herself by laughing and putting her arm around his waist. "Repeat after me, 'Mark knows what he's talking about.' Admit it!"

"It's a fair cop, Guv."

One thing she had not anticipated was the arrival of the police on Saturday morning. She sat on the couch and one of the policemen sat opposite her asking the questions. The other one remained on his feet, examining the room and peering into Sylvia's face as she answered.

"You know Paul Tedder?"

She replied hesitantly. "Yes. Not very well though."

"When did you last see him?"

"Er. Wednesday night." Careful, she told herself. They can check these sorts of things. I'll have to tell the truth.

"Where was that?"

"At the Tavern." The policeman said nothing more. She knew that he was going to let the silence force her into expanding. There had been plenty of witnesses to the events, so she might as well tell them more. "He was drunk. Very drunk. Picking an argument with the barman. I felt sorry for him so I got him a taxi."

"So you knew where he lived?"

"No. I'd only met him once before. At work. I had to go through his pockets to find his driving licence."

"So you've never been to his house?"

Sylvia hoped that there were no witnesses. She had to take that risk. "No," she replied.

"Mm." The policeman scratched his chin. "Do you know what's happened to him?"

"Yes. I heard about it. It was in yesterday's paper."

"Yet you didn't come forward."

It was a statement, not a question, but he expected a reply. "How do you mean?"

"Miss Cooper," he said in a tone that implied impatience or even disbelief. "You associate with a man who, on the next day, dies of an infectious disease and you're not concerned about yourself? You don't go to a hospital or see us?"

Sylvia hadn't thought of that. She had no answer. She decided to play dumb instead. "Put like that, it does sound awful. But I just didn't think. I've hardly had time to. I was at work all day."

"You're playing a dangerous, foolish game for an intelligent girl. But you're lucky. The experts tell us that you weren't in danger. The infectious stage had passed a few days before death apparently. And his illness may have accounted for his *appearing* drunk. He may not have been drunk at all. It could have been the last stages of the disease, according to the medical people."

"Oh." Why, Sylvia wondered, did he say that? They're trying to get the emphasis away from drunkenness, depression and suicide and onto natural illness.

"Did you meet anyone afterwards?"

The barman would have seen Mark so it was no use lying. "Yes. A friend."

"Name of. . . ?"

"Mark Little."

"I see. Did you discuss Paul Tedder?"

"A bit, yes. It's not every day I get a taxi for a drunk. I told him about it but that was the end of it."

The policeman stood up. "Okay. I think that's all we need for the moment. Thanks for your co-operation."

Thankfully, she showed them the door. Then she collapsed against it and sighed with relief. With her bare forearm she wiped her brow and found it beaded with sweat.

She nearly jumped out of her skin when someone knocked at the door. Hell, she thought, they've come back. But they hadn't. It was Derek, and she threw her arms round him. "They were police," she said. "Asking about Paul Tedder. In the Tavern."

"And you just told them the truth about what happened in the pub and nothing else, yes?" Seeing Sylvia nod, he said, "That's all right then. It'll be a routine enquiry. They're bound to do it after any death. I doubt if those two even know what they're really investigating. Anyway, it's probably the last you'll hear of it." He added, "It's a pity they saw me, though. Let's hope they didn't recognize me from my trip to the police station on account of Ellen and Jack." That was something else that hadn't occurred to her. "Sooner or later," he said, "they'll discover the connection between us anyway. That's all right, they'll see that it's simply coincidence." Sylvia hoped that he was right. She shuddered to think what would happen if the police realized that they had connected Paul Tedder's death with Ellen's, that they were concocting their own conspiracy. But if Derek was right, ordinary cops would not know Paul Tedder's true fate and there was no danger. It seemed to tally with the policemen patrolling the beach who, Mark had told her, really seemed to believe that there had been a bomb. Presumably the conspiracy was confined to the high-ups of the MoD and police. For reasons of secrecy, it seemed to make sense that they would operate in that way.

Sylvia felt calmer now but she had been unsettled by the visit. It confirmed her fear that it was very easy to make a mistake in the dangerous game of deceit that she was playing along with Mark and Derek. She just hoped that the policemen had been taken in by her display of feminine impracticality to explain her lack of concern about catching Tedder's disease. In her experience, the more macho a man was, the more likely he would expect her to be helpless, domestic and impractical. That had been her father's attitude and, she hoped, was those policemen's. Little did they know that the man whom she still pinned to the front door believed that she was the best practical worker in her year. "I tried a helpless maiden act on them," she said. "I hope it worked. I'm not good at lying."

Derek put his hands on her shoulders and pushed her away a little so he could look at her. "Somehow, I can't see you as a helpless maiden. But I'm sure that the act was fine. They've gone – and you haven't been clapped in irons. No problem." He brushed her cheek with his hand. "It's okay."

Sylvia smiled unconvincingly. "I hope so."

"I'll stay a bit if it'll help. Cheer you up."

"I wasn't going to let you go straight away anyway."

"I thought not. And I was hoping to have words with your mum. To . . . er . . . reassure her. Where is she?"

"She's not here. Gone shopping. You'll have to concentrate on cheering me up."

"And how do I do that?"

"I'll give you one guess." She lifted her face for a kiss. "Mm, when you do that," she said, "it certainly helps me to forget the police."

"So your tutor does have his uses?"

"Yes, but it's not that easy. I'm not totally cured yet."

Derek grimaced. "You're not exactly subtle either."

The kiss really did comfort her. Nothing mattered but Derek's proximity. "Better now?" he said.

"Oh, I think further treatment is required."

"Sylvia," he said as if warning a naughty school-girl against a course of action that he had read in her eyes.

"Come on, Derek. It's no use denying it." She nestled against him. "You're excited too." Derek smiled – the smile of a forced, unavoidable sub-mission.

All her problems and the stealth that now pervaded her life were submerged in a flood of calmness and happiness. She could forget chemical warfare, the dead dog, Paul Tedder, the policemen's visit. There was nothing of importance except the satisfaction of lying with Derek. She saw with pleasure that the sparkle had returned to his eyes for the first time since Ellen's death. She felt proud that she could banish the worries from his mind too. And she had been right. He *was* tender to her. With Derek, it felt natural and inevitable.

The window of the bedroom was open, letting the cool breeze billow the drawn curtains. They sat upright, Derek's arm across her bare shoulders. "Tranquil, isn't it?" he virtually whispered.

"Mm." She squeezed his hand. Then, mischiev-ously, she said, "Tell me, what were you going to reassure Mum about?"

"Oh, Sylvia. You're awful."

"But good?"

"Much too good."

* * *

Mark had expected Derek Thorn to drop in on Saturday morning to collect the sample of sand and then to head northwards straight away. Instead, he turned up with Sylvia at midday and offered to buy them both lunch before setting out on his journey. The three of them went to a small cafe in town and huddled together like gangsters for a private conversation. In hushed tones, Sylvia told Mark about being questioned by the police earlier in the day.

"Yes, it's a pity you had to tell them about me," he replied, "but I see your point. Lots of people will have seen us together in the Tavern. I'll expect a visit from the law sometime." Mark had every confidence that he could handle it. He would make sure that his story matched Sylvia's, simple as that. He himself had never even met Tedder. "Actually," he said, "I'm getting used to tackling the police. Like last night. It was easy enough to get the sand. Last time I was on the beach the policemen said they checked it on the hour, every hour. I went at twenty past twelve. I was back before one. No one saw me. Just as well," he added, "carrying a kiddy's bucket and spade after midnight."

Sylvia laughed happily. "A grown up lad like you making sandcastles at that time of night!"

"It's not a joke, Sylv," Mark retorted. He wasn't annoyed by her jibe, of course. He was annoyed

Chapter 18

Clearly, Dr Richards' secretary had a certain efficiency at putting up barriers to those with whom, she thought, Dr Richards would not wish to be encumbered.

"I assure you," Derek said, "that Dr Richards does want to speak to me."

"And I assure you that I am in a very good position to gauge his wishes. Maybe if you would tell me what you want to speak to him about?"

"I doubt very much if he would want me to discuss it with anyone else, but you could say . . . er . . . I wish to speak with him about the cover-up over Mr and Mrs Banks' deaths. Have you got that? I'd appreciate it if you used those very words. Yes?"

"Yes, I'll pass it on to him."

"Immediately." He tried to make the word sound midway between a question and a demand.

"As soon as he finishes his meeting."

"I think his proverbial meeting will be brought to an abrupt conclusion when he hears the message. Now, you have my number?"

"Yes. He'll call you back."

Derek put the telephone down and put his feet up on the desk. He did not expect to have to wait long.

He was right. His coffee was unfinished and still hot when the phone rang. "Dr Thorn?"

"Yes."

"Ah, it's Dr Richards here." The voice was trying too hard to be pleasant. "My secretary has just given me a rather bold message from you. I can't say that I understood it."

"But you called me back anyway."

"I was intrigued I must say."

Derek smiled to himself. Dr Richards was all he expected him to be – a schemer. "Let me spell it out. *I* find it intriguing that my sister, Ellen Banks, and her husband – I think you know the case – drove their car over a cliff after they had been in contact with something on Crookland Bay beach that required it to be closed."

"Specifically, Dr Thorn, what are you insinuating?"

138

Richards was trying to ascertain if Derek really did know anything damaging. Very well then. "Is it not strange, in your opinion, that an old bomb was treated with a potent tetracycline antibiotic?"

A lesser man would have hesitated on having an Achilles' heel exposed. Not Dr Richards. "Ah, yes. Now I know to what you are referring. Indeed a beach was treated in that way. It's public knowledge down here that we have had a problem with the escape of an infectious bacterium. But how do you equate that with Mr and Mrs Banks?"

"Mrs Banks called me as well as the police when she found your miscreant dog."

"I see."

"Do you want me to go on? A few words about your bacterium perhaps, and how it has been . . . manipulated?"

"All right, Dr Thorn. I think that it's time we discussed this face to face. Such conversations were not meant for the telephone."

"I agree. And tomorrow I happen to be visiting one of my students at the Forensic Laboratories on your site . . ."

"How convenient," Dr Richards interrupted.

"Indeed. Obviously we're both busy men but for this I think you'll find the time, yes?"

"Yes, I can fit you in." Their meeting was arranged for two-thirty, Thursday.

Chapter 19

Life dragged. People went about their business, unaware or uncaring of events. And Sylvia too – she acted as best she could as if nothing had happened. But the time between Derek's leaving on Saturday and his visit on Thursday seemed endless. She also had to come to terms with the fact that they would meet only at work and, in the early evening, with Mark. They would never be alone and private. Still, that was better than no visit at all. But it would be frustrating. She would be lucky if she could put herself forward for a handshake and a greeting. "Hello, Dr Thorn. Glad you could come." She was having to learn rapidly the painful restraint of an illicit lover. Would it be as painful for Derek? She didn't know. On such occasions he could mask his true feelings totally. It wasn't that he lacked emotions or feelings, Sylvia knew: he was simply giving a good performance. She was learning that the public image of Derek, the outgoing lecturer, was not his true character. He was not so self-assured as his lectures and tutorials indicated. She was pleased. She would not have fallen for a man so shallow and so secure.

In the event, it was not as bad as she had imagined. Derek engineered a thirty minute period for which they were alone – but hardly private.

When Derek arrived on Thursday he wasted no time in introducing himself to Cheryl. "You must be Dr Judson, Sylvia's supervisor."

"Yes. Cheryl Judson."

"Glad to meet you. I'm Derek Thorn." He turned to Sylvia and smiled. Not even a hand-shake, Sylvia was thinking. "Nice to see you again, Sylvia." She smiled in return but could not reply.

"Well," Cheryl asked, "how would you like to play this?"

"I don't think I'll need much of your time. How does it sound if you and I have a few minutes to make sure we're happy with the way Sylvia's settling in here, then I have a chat with Sylvia for about half an hour? I can see you both together at the end if I need to."

"Fine," Cheryl replied. "But it's no great secret that I'm pleased with the way Sylvia's applied herself. She's fitting into our team here very well."

"Good," Derek replied. "I'm sure it won't take long in that case."

It was in a quiet corner of the lab that she got Derek to herself. She looked him in the eye and saw the pain of his restraint that no one else would have spotted. They sat for a few moments in silence, appreciating each other's presence. Derek sighed. "Cheryl seems very impressed with you, Sylvia," he said, "so I haven't got a great deal to say. No pep talk needed. Just keep up the good work. But I do have to ask you to explain to me, in your own words, the work you've been doing here."

She wasn't angry. She knew that they would have to play out their roles as student and tutor, in spite of the secrets that they shared as conspirators and lovers. From time to time, he interrupted her to ask probing questions and for clarifications. After all, he'd have a report to write on her first few weeks of industrial training. Besides, she did need a tutor as well as a boyfriend. While it was hard for her to divorce one relationship from the other, she knew it was best if one did not intrude on the other. It was a distinction that she'd have to make for the next three years. It was a daunting thought. And it distracted her as she gave her account of her work. When they had finished he leaned forward, touching her forearm and said, "It *is* nice to see you again." In some ways, she wished that he hadn't. It was difficult enough, without that, to be business-like. He glanced round the laboratory, not to check if his conduct had been witnessed, but because he seemed to want to say something private. He drew his chair closer. "I told you on the phone that it was an antibiotic they used on the beach. Since then I've found out that they must be doing genetic engineering as well. I know all the chemicals and equipment they've been buying."

She nodded. "Take care, Derek. And good luck," she whispered. "Are you going to see Dr Richards straight after?"

Derek replied, "Might as well get it over with. I'll see you as arranged later. You *and* Mark."

Grieving over it would not help. They grinned at each other and Sylvia said, "Yes. And Mark made three."

So, for Sylvia's sake – for both their sakes – he had decided to contain his frustration! And how long had he upheld that decision? Only until Sylvia had applied a little pressure. In spite of his better judgement and in spite of the logic that told him to hold back, his resolve had crumbled without a fight. But it was no use mocking himself. Nothing could be undone. It *was* an irrevocable step. Derek tried to convince himself that he would undo it if he could, but renouncing something so marvellous was beyond him. He found her youth so exuberant and expressive, even now when their lives were full of conspiracies and complexities. She still had hopes, not yet dulled by the big bad world. I hope she'll still be unscarred, he thought, by the end of this business. He wasn't sure whether he was referring to their involvement in chemical warfare or their love affair. It could have been either, or both. The two had become intimately bound once Sylvia had taken refuge from one in the other. Was that all it was for her, a means of escape? No, Derek couldn't believe it. It could not have been so good between them without something more than that. Besides, looking back to her first two terms, he could now spot the first signs. They'd been there all along – well before Ellen died – but only Sylvia had seen them. He'd failed to spot them because he hadn't been looking. He hadn't considered anything beyond a good friendship. All he saw, and all he needed, was a young person with whom he'd had a lot of fun. He'd attached no significance to the fact that she happened to be female. How naive! Sylvia had been more far-sighted, more affected by his attentiveness than he'd ever intended. And now . . . he believed that she loved him. And he knew that he'd been unable to resist her because he had begun to feel the same about her.

Did their future have to be bleak? No, of course

not. Sylvia would not submit to it so why should he? Even so, Derek saw many obstacles ahead. Clearly they had become embroiled with the dubious activities of Crookland Bay Research Centre but that was not the only threat to them. Crossing swords with the MoD was simply danger-ous to them both, the other barriers were more subtle and more likely to come between them. Guilt. Derek remembered how guilty he had felt over his helplessness in investigating Ellen's death. Now he was adding yet more guilt. What would he be called? A baby-snatcher? Hardly. Even if he was eleven years her senior. She was old enough to decide for herself and they had done nothing illegal. No, it was not their ages that jarred but the fact that she was his student, his pupil. He was respon-sible for her at the university. He was there to oversee her education in life. He felt as if he had betrayed some great principle when he saw what she was learning from him. Then there was Sylvia's mother who, it seemed, preferred Mark. And Mark himself. He was perhaps the biggest obstacle of all. A boyfriend – or ex-boyfriend – who was clearly still keen, very keen, on Sylvia could hardly be pleased with this latest turn of events. But despite all the barriers to their relationship Derek could not help himself. No other woman had ever meant more to him than Sylvia did now. He needed her youth and her attitude. And he needed to touch her. Even in the forensic lab, he could not resist it. No matter how brief the touch, it boosted him for his meeting with Richards. He hoped, through touch, to acquire a little of her youthful optimism.

Richards' office was large and plush. Five times the size of Derek's own meagre room back at the university. Richards himself was a big man, somewhat taller than Derek, and about forty-five, Derek guessed. He was clean-shaven, immaculate in dress and brimming with courtesy. An Oxford man, no doubt. Probably a confirmed bachelor. He waved Derek towards the small but comfortable chair in front of the imposing desk. "Sherry?" he asked.

Derek refused. He knew that Richards was trying to make him feel indebted for the comforts offered. He knows all the tricks, Derek thought. I bet that when he sits behind his desk I'll be looking up to him, perched on a chair much taller than mine. He smiled to himself. He had not expected anything other than Richards to pull rank on him.

"Now," Richards said, at last taking his seat and peering down on Derek, "what was it you wanted to say to me?"

Behind Richards a smattering of rain obscured the view over the sea which today had lost much of its lustre. Derek was glad that it was now uncompromisingly grey and unfriendly. He needed an enemy to remind him of his anger amidst Richards' pleasantries. Anyway, he did not want the distraction of a view behind Richards. He wanted to be looking him directly in the face. "I want to hear your version of the events leading to the deaths of Ellen and Jack Banks," Derek said bluntly.

"From our telephone conversation, it appears that you have your own version already. I have to confess that you have found us out. It's said that our sins always catch up with us, isn't it? But I don't want to turn this into a confrontation between us. Let me explain." He opened his hands, a gesture intended to mean that he was going to bare his soul. "As I said to you, we had an accident – not of our own making – here in our Biology Department which resulted in the escape of a fatal bacterium."

Derek interrupted, hoping to unsettle him somewhat. "The carrier being a dog?"

"Yes. It . . ."

"How did it end up in the sea?"

"That's a matter I'd rather leave at the moment."

"Presumably via the two CAR protesters."

"Why do you say that?"

"The locals tell me that from the day of the CAR break-in till when Ellen and Jack stumbled across the dog, there were helicopter searches of the beach."

Richards shrugged. "Two and two *does* make four."

"The only thing I don't understand about that,

is how the protesters only contaminated them-selves. Why wasn't this site infected and closed off like the beach?"

"The dog was in a sealed bag, of course. As they made off with it, they gave the bag more rough treatment than it was designed for. When they realized that they couldn't escape with the dog, they threw it into the sea. At that point the bag split. One of them touched the dog's leg and the other was close enough. Our security staff saw what happened and hence didn't approach them unprotected. Both the CAR members were isolated immediately. The only threat was to themselves and whoever found the dog."

"What about sea life?"

"The disease is fairly selective. Certainly fish and birds are not affected."

"I see. Well, as you suggested, let's leave that," Derek said, "and carry on from when my sister and her husband did find the dog."

"They were infected by the disease that the dog was carrying. I'm sorry that I have to say that it is not a pleasant death. As if any is. We did every-thing for them, you understand," Richards added quickly. "There would have been no pain. We decided it better not to confront the public with such a death and, at the same time, undermine the confidence we have painstakingly built up. Hence, I'm afraid, our rather clumsy act of deception."

It didn't come as a shock to him. If anything it was a relief to have it confirmed officially but he did not let Richards see that relief. "So you decided that not even her closest relative should hear the truth? Presumptuous, wasn't it?"

"We didn't know then your good character. With hindsight, things would have been different."

Derek thought it was about time that the conversation did become a confrontation. He looked Richards in the eye and said, "Perhaps I could forgive you that – for the sake of the poor public – if it weren't for the fact that you're still not telling the full story."

"Ah," Richards replied. "Now, as on the telephone yesterday, you do have me at a disadvantage."

"You've already guessed that I analysed a sample of sand from your 'bomb site' but I wouldn't have done that if I hadn't been alerted by something else. I found out that your Biology Department was doing some genetic engineering . . ."

"How do you come to that conclusion?"

Good. He interrupted, Derek thought. He's a little rattled. "I received an invoice from Downs Chemicals the other day for one of my own purchases. One of your invoices had been included by accident."

"What a coincidence! Still, I don't wish to dwell on such 'coincidences'. By one means or another, you have discovered that we buy certain chemicals and equipment. I must suggest to Downs that their confidentiality could be ... improved. Anyway, you came to what conclusion?"

"Come now, Dr Richards. This is a Ministry of Defence research establishment and I'm no fool. Your bacterium has been engineered to produce a toxin. It is no doubt a very effective agent for chemical warfare."

Richards nodded slowly. He rose and peered out through the window. Then he turned to Derek and said, "I won't do you the disservice of denying it. Despite the leap in logic between genetic engineering – which I admit – and CBW. You're an intelligent man who's done a little research on us. And you've found out more than most ever get to know about us. That means you now share our burdens."

"Burdens?" Derek queried.

"Yes. Of secrecy. It is strange that something we should all be proud of has to be secret." Richards smiled, for the first time revealing unpleasantness, at the corners of his mouth. "I see by your face that we do not see eye to eye on this matter. You do not approve. But perhaps your research has extended to the legalities of the situation so that you know that we are within international law. And, of course, that *all* our work is purely defensive."

"Yes, I know that. And I still deplore it. I wish

that production and stockpiling of chemical weapons, as well as their use, were banned. And we should renounce the right to retaliate in kind. Make your work – defensive or not – redundant. Until that's done, we'll never have security against chemical warfare."

"But that isn't true," Richards argued. "Our efforts here in this institute guarantee that chemical weapons won't be used in a major conflict. Don't get me wrong when I say that I'm proud. I'm not proud that our research is necessary. I wish it wasn't. No. I'm proud that we can keep the peace by making it too dangerous for anyone to attack us with a chemical weapon. For fear of reprisal. That is the essence of strong defence."

"But you've amply demonstrated in the last few weeks that accidents can occur. What if it hadn't just been an infected dog that they took but a culture of the bug itself? Presumably even a brief exposure to the atmosphere would mean much more than closing this site or a bit of beach."

Richards looked hard at him for a moment. Then he gave a concessionary smile. "A tender spot, Dr Thorn. But we have learned. Security has been tightened. It will not happen again. What interests me," he said, changing the subject, "is what you hoped to gain by coming here. Obviously to lay your sister's ghost – if you'll forgive my expression – but what else? Surely you're not going to say that you hoped to put a stop to our necessarily unsavoury research? You're not as naive as those CAR members."

Any triumph that Derek might have felt by extracting Richards' admissions soon evaporated. He could not even argue against Richards. Both of them knew all the arguments. And whilst they remained largely unresolved, Derek knew that the authorities would err on the side of caution, that the weapons would be investigated – just in case. It was no good to plead some sense of moral wrong-doing. Richards would agree that it was regrettable – but necessary. If Derek argued that the money would be better spent on health and education, Richards would claim that health and education would be irrelevant if as a result we suffered attack by chemical weapons. Derek felt impotent. He had achieved nothing.

"The public – at least the majority of it – lives happily with our nuclear weapons," Richards was saying. "The public might be appalled initially by the capabilities of CBW but people would soon realize that it was just another necessary evil in the world today. They would live with our Research Station just as they live with the Atomic Weapons Research Establishment. Besides, you'll soon realize that you can do nothing with your extra knowledge, Dr Thorn. We have an . . . arrangement with the press, and so on. Anyway," he added with emphasis, "you're not so sure that you're right as to endanger the disarmament talks by spilling the beans. Even if there were a mechanism whereby they might be spilled."

Derek knew that Richards had read uncertainty in his face. "But," he counteracted, "if you're so right, how does knowledge endanger the Geneva talks?"

"Good question," Richards responded. "The delegates have an inkling of our capabilities. We want them to have an inkling. That's why they're keen for disarmament. But for a nation taking a strong lead in the talks, wide knowledge of our work would be embarrassing. It would be used against us by unfriendly politicians because there's another type of war that politicians love to win even more than the real thing – the propaganda war. A nation discredited in the eyes of the masses is *not* one that's going to have a real impact in disarmament talks."

"You know," Derek said as he got up to leave, "I don't think you'd like it if your research ever became unnecessary, if we really disarmed. You're enjoying the game too much."

So it had gone exactly as he expected. Derek Thorn had got Richards to admit to everything – apart from Tedder's suicide, a subject Thorn had not raised – but failed to do anything at all about it. It was up to him, Mark, to achieve something worthwhile. He had been thinking about it since the weekend. There were at least three things he could try. Three plans he would try. He was not like this Dr Thorn, all talk and no action. Mind you, he was better equipped for action than Derek Thorn. Not even Sylvia knew how well equipped he was. Mark was glad he'd gone back to Tedder's house that night. Armed with the suicide note and the T42, he could have Richards and the whole Crookland Bay Research Station at his mercy. He could achieve anything he wanted with such weapons.

Chapter 20

"Charles. I have a suggestion for you," Dr Richards said to his old friend, now the region's Chief Inspector.

"Yes, George?"

"Dr Derek A. Thorn. I'll give you his work address in a moment. He's the brother of Ellen Banks. Remember? We ought to keep an eye on him. By that, I mean you ought to assign someone to him. Maybe from the Midlands Police Force since he lives in Coventry. I don't believe for one moment that he has – or even knows about – our missing substance. He's too responsible for that. But he should not be overlooked. He has been down here on a number of occasions, seeing one of his students at the forensic labs here at Crookland

Bay. I checked it out. And who should she be but our Miss Sylvia Cooper. She's the one who got Tedder home in the taxi, isn't she?"

"Yes. It's most interesting. And unfortunate. As you say, worth keeping an eye on. But I must say, George, that *I* could tell *you* all about Dr Thorn. Thanks to an astute local bobby. You see, we've been keeping an eye on Sylvia Cooper since Saturday. We weren't totally satisfied with Miss Cooper's version of events. I won't go into it on the phone but her behaviour was not really consistent with her account. Anyway, one of my men recognized Derek Thorn on Saturday when he visited Cooper. We've had our eye on him, as you put it, since then. And yesterday, after his meeting with you, he saw another of our friends, Mark Little, along with Cooper. I imagine they were comparing notes. You must let me know what you said to our Dr Thorn."

"Basically, he's managed to piece together more than we would like him to, presumably with help from Sylvia Cooper. But we cannot put a stop to an inquisitive mind, Charles."

"Did he ask you about Tedder at all?"

"No. Presumably he wasn't on firm ground there. He presented me only with those aspects on which he had solid facts. The death of the Banks and the CAR members, and our own research in CBW. He knows the truth about all of those."

"Mm. So last night, they'll have worked out how Tedder fitted in. But on what level we don't know. We have no evidence at all that they know anything more than that he died due to an accident in the lab."

"Let's hope so."

"Under the circumstances, their liaison is probably fairly harmless but we'll maintain our vigilance."

"There's still nothing to link them with the missing substance?"

"More than that, there's no evidence to link it with Tedder."

"Apart from my chemists' intuition."

"Hardly evidence, George!"

George Richards grinned. "I know. Anyway, I have an idea concerning Dr Thorn."

"Oh, yes?"

"Yes. As to how I might keep him off our backs. How *I* can exert a little pressure on *him*."

Chapter 21

Furtively, Mark peered out from behind the curtain and checked again on the man who was tending the verge opposite. Even for a council worker on a Friday afternoon, he was taking too long over it. Smiling, Mark turned away from the window. He could hazard a very good guess as to what was going on. He never did have that visit from the police. Instead, they had elected to keep him under surveillance. Hence, the "council workman" opposite and the man who followed Mark to and from school. In one way, the surveillance was reassuring. It told him that the police had not yet connected him with Paul Tedder. Otherwise, they would not be out there gathering information on him still. No, they would have hauled him off by now if they really knew anything. From now on, he told himself, he would have to be very careful. That was the awkward part of having watchdogs on your heels.

Right now, the surveillance was a nuisance because he didn't know if it extended to the telephone. He had skived off school for the afternoon to make a call but didn't know if the police would go to the extent of tapping his telephone. He decided against using it just in case. Yet, knowing that he would be followed, telephoning from a call box would be too suspicious. He had confidence that, with his knowledge of the network of lanes that was Crookland Bay, he could give the policeman the slip but that too would arouse suspicion. He wanted to reserve that action for possible future use – if it became necessary. No, the best bet was to go to a friend's house, someone who was not connected at all with this business, and ask to use his telephone. Mark could claim that his own phone was temporarily out of action. Tom Williams. He was the prime candidate. He'd been in the same year as Sylvia and Mark but left school at sixteen. He was still unemployed so he'd probably be at home. And his sole interest was, and always had been, in things female. He would not be curious about a clandestine phone call on the topic of chemical warfare. His one-track mind would not be able to cope with it.

The ploy worked. The plain-clothes man who waited outside Tom Williams' house must have been blissfully unaware of Mark's activity and Tom himself disinterestedly left Mark in the hall to make his call in private.

It took two attempts and several hints about a big story on Crookland Bay Research Station to get to speak to someone in authority. Eventually, a man's voice came on the line saying, "Hello. Yes, I'm the Features Editor. Ron Simpson by name. What can I do for you, Mr Wrightson? I gather it's about CBRS, as we call it here."

Mark had taken a leaf out of Derek Thorn's book and used a pseudonym. He did not wish to be traced afterwards if they wouldn't print his story. "Well, you'll know then that it's a place where the MoD does its research," he replied.

"Believe me, Mr Wrightson, I have in front of me a file on that particular institution as thick as your telephone directory. I took the precaution of digging out the file before coming to the phone. Actually, it didn't require much digging. We've been adding to it quite a lot over the last three weeks. Various events down there have attracted much publicity, haven't they?"

"Oh, you don't know the half of it," Mark said.

The editor seemed to take a modicum of offence and replied sharply, "Are you sure about that? Our investigative journalists do know what they're doing, Mr Wrightson. But let's not jump the gun. Tell me what you've got on our esteemed MoD institute."

Mark was disorientated by the man's tone of voice which varied with extraordinary rapidity between flippancy and impatience. Putting his reservations aside, Mark narrated his story. He detailed the photographs of the dog, Ellen and Jack Banks, and Tedder's suicide note but he did not mention the missing T42. He did not want to play all his aces at once. He fell silent and waited for the editor to respond, to do what he must to clear the centre pages of the newspaper for Mark's story. The editor gave a short cough then said, "That's extremely interesting, Mr Wrightson. What's your real name, by the way?"

Mark snorted. Just what did this editor think he was trying to do? Unnerve him? Test him in some way? "Wrightson will do," he snapped.

"Okay, if that's how you want to play it. Now, as to your story, it's filled in a lot of blanks for us. Especially on Tedder's role. We were in two minds about him. Whether he was a martyr to a cause or simply someone in the wrong place at the wrong time, an unfortunate accident as the MoD claimed."

Mark was stunned. "So you know all about it?"

"Apart from the gaps you've just filled in for us, yes. For instance, we didn't know that they called their weapon T42. Don't be surprised," he added,

"I told you that my reporters are not fools. We've kept an eye on CBRS since its inception years and years ago. Given the recent nasty goings-on in Crookland Bay, we'd guessed what's happening."

"So why haven't you printed the story?" Astonishment was clear in Mark's tone.

"Don't let's be naive, Mr Wrightson. The free press is not that free. There's a little gem of a law called the Official Secrets Act, you know. We can't publish all we'd like to publish, and being sensational isn't the only criterion for a newspaper story. You see, you've stumbled on just one example of officialdom working in wondrous ways. There are many others. There are strict controls on reporting of such matters. It's one thing to leak a few Whitehall secrets. Many of those are meant to be leaked anyway. But it's another thing altogether when national security is involved. The powers that be take a very dim view of those sorts of leaks. I've no desire to end a brilliant career in prison."

"But I've got photographs to prove it. And Tedder's suicide note. Aren't you interested in those?"

"Indeed I am. I'd love to see your pretty pictures. For our file . . ."

"Damn your file," Mark retorted. "I could even get hold of some T42. Wouldn't that change your mind? To show that their security is hopeless."

"I think, Mr Wrightson, that we should call a

halt to this conversation before you get carried away. Or, if I was honest, maybe because you scare me. Believe me, I cannot print the story – however much I'd like to. We can publish only what CBRS tells us. So there's no point in your contemplating something foolish on this newspaper's behalf. Or on anyone else's."

"And what if I told you that some T42 has gone missing already?"

There was a silence before the editor replied. "Then I would pray for both of us. That is the only thing I could do."

"Well, there's nothing else for us to say then, is there? Thank you for all your help, I'm sure."

"Don't bear a grudge, lad. The world's not against you specifically. It's against us all."

Mark put the receiver down and swore.

"I heard that!" Tom said, passing through the hall on the way to the kitchen. "You should stick to women – they don't give you so much aggro. Not usually, anyhow."

"Oh yes?" Mark didn't really feel like talking but could not be ungracious for the use of Tom's telephone.

"Do I detect doubt? That girl of yours – she of the outstanding structure – is she playing you up?"

"No. Everything's fine."

"You might be the envy of the lads at school but not of me. I remember her from year ten. I hope for your sake that she's thawed out a bit since then."

"No comment." Mark put just enough innuendo in his voice for Tom's sake. It implied, "Thawed? She's red hot now." They might call him Tom now rather than Tommy but he was still the same irrepressible boaster of sexual prowess that he had been in year ten. Mark felt that his own relationship with Sylvia, which had blossomed from childhood friendship to romance in that same year at school, was on a higher plane than any to which Tom could aspire. At least it had been until Thorn's arrival on the scene. But it was still too precious to be discussed with Tom Williams. Mark thanked him for the use of his telephone and left.

It was as plain as day that Sylvia was having an affair with Derek Thorn. The self-satisfied look on his face – on both their faces – last Saturday had confirmed it, yet Mark had no intention of just giving up. He would win her back from this college lecturer. Sylvia wanted action over Crookland Bay's chemical warfare establishment. Action was something he could provide, not Dr Thorn. If only the damn press wasn't so scared of D-notices. Perhaps CAR would not be so cautious. Perhaps they would help him get the kind of publicity that Paul Tedder had failed to attract. Mark had hoped to ring CAR at Tom Williams' house but could not face further conversation about Sylvia. He had evaded Tom Williams, now he must evade also the man in the blue cagoule who strolled nonchalantly behind him and had done ever since he'd left his own house. Mark did not want to act as if he knew he was being followed. It would have to look natural. He headed for the nearest bus route into town. It shouldn't be too difficult – just a matter of timing. His spine tingled at the prospect of the challenge.

On the main coast road into Crookland Bay, Mark stood at a view point, looking out to sea but keeping the corner of his eye on the road. The policeman had stopped some distance away, also viewing the sea. When the bus appeared, Mark's heart began to pound. At what point should he run? Careful, he told himself. Judge it well.

Suddenly he looked up and noticed the bus, as if for the first time. He glanced at his watch, pretending that the bus was unexpectedly early. Then he sprinted to the bus-stop, waving to the driver to stop. What, he thought, if there are lots of people waiting to get off the bus at this stop? The policeman, who had also broken into a run, would be able to catch the bus too. But Mark saw with relief that no one wanted to alight. He jumped onto the platform and the driver accelerated away immediately. Sitting on the bus, recovering from the excitement, he refrained from looking back to see the reactions of the policeman. Mark smiled, he would have loved to have seen that man's face.

He got off the bus as soon as he saw a payphone. The thrill of losing his watchdog policeman was waning. He was left with a feeling of nervousness as he remembered how his last call had ended in failure. It was a failure that he found difficult to accept because he had expected the journalist to snap up his story immediately. This time he would be more cautious in his approach. He checked the newspaper clipping in his pocket for the name of the CAR spokesman who had been so derogatory about the MoD research station. He had already taken the precaution of looking up the telephone number of the CAR headquarters in the reference library. The telephone did not ring for long. "Hello. Campaign for Animal Rights," a female voice said.

"Hello. Can I speak to Gregory Drake, please?"

"Just a minute. I'll check if he's in. Who's calling?"

"Well, he doesn't know me but I'm calling about the CAR members who died at Crookland Bay."

"I see. Who is it speaking?"

"Mark Wrightson. I'm in a public phone actually, so if you could hurry . . ."

"Okay. Just a moment."

Mark could hear voices but could not make out what was being said. Then a man's voice came on the line. "Gregory Drake speaking." It was a congenial, fairly young voice. Its tone heartened Mark. "I'd like to give you some information about Crookland Bay Research Station," Mark replied. "And the CAR protesters who died there."

"I'm all ears, Mr. . . ?"

"Wrightson. Mark Wrightson. Are you aware of the type of work that goes on there?"

"Yes. They infect animals with various diseases so they can experiment with various trial treatments, basically. At least, that's the part that interests us."

"Well, it's not that simple," Mark said. The small pile of coins in front of him dwindled in size as Mark described the work carried out, emphasizing the relationship between Paul Tedder's tip-off about the dog and the deaths of the CAR members. He was interrupted only by the pips; Gregory Drake listened in silence.

"That's some story, Mr Wrightson," the CAR spokesman said when Mark had finished. "Knowing the MoD, I believe every word."

"So you're willing to help?"

"In what way?"

"Expose them – and the various cover-ups."

Gregory Drake took a few moments to consider. "I have a lot of sympathy with you and with what you're trying to do but I can't see how we can help. To be honest, my main concern is the aim of this organization, CAR. To publicize and thereby end cruelty to animals in laboratories. Crookland Bay Research Station is just one organization on our black list. If we were to throw the weight of CAR behind you, we'd be diluting the issue of animal rights." He spoke carefully and articulately. "To focus the public attention on just one specific – and no doubt uncommon – practice would, if anything, detract from our campaign because it would concentrate the public's mind on an altogether different issue, that of chemical warfare. I really am sorry to say this so bluntly to you but I hope you understand."

"What about your two members who died? Don't you care about them – especially when the MoD is blaming you, CAR, for their deaths?"

"Injustice comes in all shapes and sizes, doesn't it? But we do care. A lot. We've pressed for an inquest on Robert Noon and John Davis. Given, though, that the only material witnesses will be MoD officials and military doctors, I think that we can guess the outcome. In any event I'll certainly make sure that all CAR members know how they really died. That is of paramount importance but it doesn't change the cause for which they died."

Maybe the CAR spokesman was being more sympathetic than the journalist, but the answer was the same. "This chemical warfare acts on animals as well as humans," Mark objected. "They test it out on animals as well." Outside the telephone box, an elderly lady was waiting, looking alternately at Mark and her watch. Mark turned to one side so he could not see her off-putting glances.

"I appreciate that, Mr Wrightson. Let me put it another way. To us at CAR, drugs and cosmetics are chemical weapons in the hands of animal experimenters. Weapons that are used to injure and kill thousands of living creatures every day. It's that chemical warfare that we intend to stop. It may be more mundane than the MoD work you've out-lined but, in terms of sheer numbers, it accounts for the vast majority of laboratory cruelty. It's in the name of shampoos, lipsticks and cigarettes that animals are being maimed and killed – that's our message to the public. As nasty as it is, the work at Crookland Bay Research Station does not add par-ticularly to cruelty to animals when the whole gamut of laboratory experimentation is considered. I must stress again," he added, "that I approve of your motives but, in my capacity here at CAR, my hands are tied. I could not do CAR the disservice of backing you."

Mark had lost faith in others. First Derek Thorn, then the press, and now CAR. After the pips had sounded yet again, he neither spoke nor used another coin. He left, holding open the door of the booth for the impatient lady. Mark did not notice her scowling at him as she entered.

He guessed that he now knew how Paul Tedder had felt – helpless. They say that suicide is a cry for help, Mark thought. His next action, like Paul Tedder's, would be drastic. The difference between them was that Mark would not cry for help. He would go it alone. Not suicide. That was too simple and it would play into the MoD's hands. No, plan three was much more sophisticated than suicide – and it would challenge Dr Richards and his research station directly. That was the element missing from Paul Tedder's scheme. Mark would not make such a mistake. As he walked through the outskirts on his way home, it began to drizzle. He muttered to himself, quoting from Tedder's suicide note, "It's going to rain soon."

The reaction of the "council worker" when Mark returned to his house was the only thing that brightened the otherwise dull afternoon. He rushed to a clean and surprisingly expensive parked car. Inside it, he was no doubt communicating with headquarters, ending the panic over Mark's whereabouts. Mark allowed himself a grin. Hardly the most subtle of actions! He hoped that the policeman who had been following him was being given a good dressing down for losing him.

Up in his bedroom that evening, Mark drew a piece of paper towards him, but the precise words he wanted did not come to him. He addressed the envelope instead. Dr Richards, Crookland Bay

Research Station, Crookland Bay, Devon. Mark wondered where he would be when he posted it, the most important letter of his life. Location still required some thought. It would be no trouble to get away. At night, a policeman lounged in a car outside the house so he could see both the front and side doors. Mark had never seen anyone watching from the back. Either the police were short of manpower or they were sufficiently confident – or conceited – to think that Mark had not spotted their surveillance. The patio door that opened onto the back garden was invitingly hidden from the policeman's view. That route to the beach and sea had been a friend to him before. Now that he was to be a fugitive, it would be a friend again.

He put the paper to one side. He could write the letter tomorrow. For now, he had to sort out a few things – clothes, money, train times. Later on, he would escape unseen over the familiar territory at the back of the house. It would all be over in time for half-term, revision, then "A" levels next month.

Fridays were living up to their bad reputation. It was exactly two weeks ago that he'd walked along Crookland Bay coast to find the closed-off beach. Last Friday, he'd gone back to Crookland Bay to hear from Sylvia and Mark just how murky the whole episode had become. This Friday, Derek was trying to work on as if nothing at all was happening outside the university. But he found it increasingly difficult. His whole life had become consumed with events in Crookland Bay – and that included Sylvia.

The telephone rang. An internal call.

"Derek?"

"Yes, Ian," he replied, recognizing the Head of Department's voice. "What can I do for you?"

"You can come down to my office."

"Now?"

"Right now. We have a couple of items to discuss urgently."

Derek was taken aback. Never before had he heard that tone from Ian – not aimed at a member of staff anyway. Derek put down the phone, saluted it and said aloud, "Yes, sir!"

"Ah, Derek," Ian said. "Thanks for coming. Shut the door. Have a seat." The seat by the Head of Department's desk was extremely uncomfortable. It was said that Ian had never done anything about the chair because he liked its occupant to be at a disadvantage. Students particularly feared the chair, staff had merely to put up with it. "You wanted to see me?" Derek asked.

"Yes. A couple of items, actually. I've had a rather alarming call about you. I'm not going into details. However, I do feel that it's time I reminded a young member of staff like yourself of . . . how shall I put it? . . . the facts of life as far as this department is concerned." Ian adjusted the papers on his desk, to give himself time to think. "The strong reputation of this department rests heavily on its research which in turn depends on continued MoD funding. I'd be failing in my duty if I let anything come between this department and the MoD. Do you see what I am saying? I've had to placate the MoD and give certain assurances about my staff here."

Derek nodded slowly, not to signify his agreement with, but his understanding of, the comments. He should have foreseen this, of course. He had put pressure on Richards. In turn, Richards was bound to put pressure on him. And what better way than through the department? Obviously, Richards had checked out the degree of MoD funding of work in Derek's department. Because of its high level, Richards was able to recruit Ian to his side. "Point taken," Derek said. "What's the other matter?"

"I was going to see you about this at the end of last term but there wasn't a convenient moment. Anyway, I hoped it would cool off during the first industrial training period. But now we're in the mood, I might as well raise the issue to ensure that it *does* cool off before the students return next term." He paused before explaining, "I approve fully of staff getting to know their personal tutees. It makes for harmonious staff-student relationships.

But there is a limit. It has been noted that you have an unusual relationship with Miss Cooper."

"Noted from where?" Derek queried.

"Oh, here and there."

"For example?"

"An overheard conversation between students in the laboratories."

"You're listening to students' rumours now?"

"I know. If I acted on all they said in their vindictive moments about the lecturing ability of my staff, I'd have to sack half of them. But you're a popular member of staff. They wouldn't be malicious about you, so . . ."

"So you believe it."

"Are you denying it?"

"No," Derek replied. "I won't deny that our relationship is unusually cordial."

Ian shook his head. "Look. All I have to say is that it is rather unwise in your now precarious situation to be seen to have an improper affinity to a female student."

"So what do you want me to say?"

"I don't want a response at all. I want you to consider what I've said and take appropriate action. Or inaction, perhaps. Anyway, I don't wish to hear any more about it, not from the MoD, from yourself, or about Sylvia Cooper. You sort it out, Derek."

"Okay," Derek replied. "I'll do what I think is

right." On his way out, he closed the door behind him and muttered, "Bloody Fridays!"

Mrs Cooper put down her sewing and turned off the television. Sylvia looked with trepidation at her. There was barely ten minutes to go before her mother's favourite Friday evening programme. It meant that there was something important on her mind, something they had to discuss.

"Sylvia," she began, "I'm not so daft that I don't know when my daughter's having an affair."

It came like a bombshell, despite all the warning signs. The television, the way she always started a difficult conversation with her daughter's name. Then straight to the heart of the matter, no punches pulled. There did not seem much point in denying it. "Affair makes it sound dirty. But it's not, Mum."

"You said you've dropped Mark because he was only after a bit of excitement. What was it you said? A status symbol. Well, you haven't yet learned, my girl, that men don't change. Do you think this Dr Thorn is any different? He's after excitement too – a status symbol of a different sort."

"That's not true, Mum. Derek's . . ."

Her mother interrupted. "Derek's trying to re-capture the youthful excitement that Mark still has. He's trying to recapture his own youth, to show he can still get the girls."

"He's not, Mum. You don't know him. And he's not that old anyway."

"He's too old for you for a start. You just watch. He's made his conquest – soon he'll lose interest."

Sylvia stared in horror at her mother. How could she say that? "It's not like that, I promise."

"So you can honestly tell me that he loves you?"

Sylvia hesitated. Her mother would know if she lied so she told the truth. "I don't know. Maybe he does. Maybe he will. I only know that we like each other a lot and want to be together." Her face showed recalcitrance but in her mother's she saw only disagreement. "What have you got against him, exactly?" she asked.

"He's too old for you."

"You're exaggerating," she interrupted. "He's only thirty, maybe less."

"Maybe more. He'll certainly be over forty when you're thirty. That's too old. Anyway, he should not be cavorting with his female students." She put up her hand, "Don't interrupt. Believe me, Sylvia, I'm thinking of your own good. So hear me out. Because there's Mark to consider as well. He's no fool. He'll know how far it's gone. And I don't want you – or this Dr Thorn – to hurt Mark any more than you have already. He loves you, you know. Very much. He's jealous and possessive too. He won't give you up so easily."

"Is that a good reason for loving Mark, though, because he dotes on me?"

Her mother shrugged. "Do you think you'll do any better with Derek Thorn?"

"Yes." She stood up to leave the room. "Definitely."

"Don't walk out on me this time, Sylvia. I'm trying to pass on to you the wisdom of someone who's seen more years than you have. I just want what's best for you. I've heard too many tales with sorry endings about young women who fell for much older men."

"You're exaggerating again!"

Her mother shook her head sadly. "He really has seduced you."

"Mum!" Sylvia cried. "It wasn't . . . isn't like that. You haven't even met him." An idea struck her that helped to calm her down. "Why don't you meet him? He'd come down this weekend if I asked him to."

"No, I don't want to meet him. That would be like an official sanction."

"Mum, I don't need official sanction any more. I've a good mind to phone him anyway. I'd like to see him this weekend."

"As you rightly point out," her mother replied, "I can't stop you. But be careful. You know what I'm talking about. Whatever you think, it's you I care about."

*   *   *

"Hello? Sylvia Cooper speaking."

"It's Derek here."

"Oh, Derek. I'm glad you phoned. I was going to call you."

"Oh, yes? What about?"

Sylvia lowered her voice even though she would have claimed that she did not care whether her mother heard or not. "Earlier tonight I had another . . . discussion with Mum. About you."

"And I've had a discussion with my Head of Department about you."

"Oh?"

"The HoD has heard rumours about us – and he doesn't like it. Ironically, it was last term when we were pure and innocent. But I had my wrist slapped anyway!"

He did not sound too disconsolate about it but maybe it was an act designed so that she would not feel bad about it. "You haven't been sacked or anything?"

"No." He gave a chuckle. "Nothing so drastic. It would have to be the Principal's underage daughter – or wife – to merit that."

"But you're calling because of it?"

"That, and wanting to hear you again. I'm not running scared of the HoD but things do seem to be hotting up – in the worst possible sense – for both of us. I think it's time we had a chat about it. Not just over the phone either. It's a good excuse to see you again. This weekend if it's okay with you. Yes?"

"Yes. Of course. I'd love it. A dirty weekend as Mr and Mrs Smith. But where?"

"Not the whole weekend, Sylvia. Just tomorrow. Remember what we've got to talk through. Let's make it a lunch and afternoon somewhere. I know what you earn at the forensic labs so I won't ask you to come up here. It's too expensive."

"It's all right," Sylvia interrupted. "There's a train . . ."

"I think some neutral ground would be preferable."

"Neutral ground?"

"Well, how about Exeter? I can drive down, if you can get there easily as well."

"Yes. No problem." Sylvia noted down Derek's instructions on where they could meet in Exeter at about lunch-time. "Just one question," she added. "Since I'm meeting my tutor, do you think the university will pay my travelling expenses?"

Derek laughed. "I'm meeting my student but they won't pay mine."

Chapter 22

"Disappeared? How do you mean?"

"It must have been last night. There's quite a commotion at the house this morning. The parents, you know."

"And McGregor didn't see his departure?" Charles asked.

"No. He must have realized McGregor was watching him and gone out of the back. It was always a risk, that. But we don't think we could have prevented it anyway. If Mark Little wanted to escape our notice in the dead of night on his home territory, he would have done so, even with a man at the back of the house."

"I agree. I'm not blaming McGregor or yourself, Sergeant. Let's think of what we're going to do about it." Charles paused. "I hardly need to tell you to cart his picture around the coach and train stations and so on. If he took transport at that time of night, he'd be very noticeable. And put out a nationwide call in case he's hitchhiking. But no press or TV coverage at this stage. His parents will come to you to report him missing. That'll be sometime today, I imagine. If they don't, then he must have left them a note or discussed it with them. That will be trickier to handle. Keep me posted. Assuming they do report him missing, check his financial position. Access to bank accounts or whatever. Also, get a prints man into his house. If his parents query it, tell them it's standard procedure. Having fingerprints helps in the search for him, okay?" Charles did not wait for a reply. He continued, "Check if his prints match any found at Paul Tedder's house. Got that?"

"Yes. Paul Tedder – the one who died through the MoD infectious outbreak. You mean there's a connection between Tedder and Little, sir?"

"Check the fingerprints then you tell me, Sergeant. Remember, though, that the level of confidentiality applied to the Tedder case now applies to Mark Little's. Now," he added, "you can't do my weekend much more harm than you already have, so keep me informed even if it's midnight tonight or tomorrow when you have some news."

"Yes, sir," came the deferential reply.

Chapter 23

The kiss with which Derek greeted Sylvia told her that he did love her. It took away any shred of doubt. He held her tight, as if to prevent Mark, her mum or his boss at the university coming between them. Sylvia, her head on his shoulder, smiled to herself. "Hey," she said. "I'm not sure Exeter is ready for this."

Derek drew away from her somewhat, and looked around. "Are we getting an audience?"

"The opposite," she replied. "They're all trying not to look."

"Suddenly," he said, kissing her again, "I don't care."

She grinned at him. "But would you do it in the bar at college?"

"Spoil-sport!" He let her go. "Come on. Let's get some lunch before we talk shop. There's a place just down the road and on the left somewhere, as I recall. They serve a nifty Greek meal."

"A reminder of your student days here, no doubt."

"That's right." His arm gripped her around the waist and pulled her whole body against his as they walked through the drizzle to the restaurant. There was a shock, though, when they got there. "Oh, no!" Derek exclaimed. "It's a pizza place now!"

Sylvia laughed. "That's progress for you."

"Hadn't even heard of pizzas in my day."

"You poor old man," Sylvia mocked. "Anyway it doesn't matter. Let's go in. Perhaps they do a kebab pizza."

"Well," Derek said, as they tucked into a giant pizza between them, "we've got to talk about it sometime."

Sylvia didn't ask what they had to talk about. She knew. She didn't reply but waited for him to say more.

"When your mum disapproves and my boss gets heavy, it just makes me more determined. The rebellious streak comes out in me, and I think, 'Sod them. We're enjoying ourselves, not doing anything wrong.' But am I being pig-headed just to spite them? Maybe we're getting some good advice really. Advice that's childish to ignore." He sighed. "I'm not used to bowing to pressure but there's some sense in it, I'm afraid."

"You want us to become student and tutor again."

"I don't think 'want' is the right word. What I want can't be done in a pizza place."

Despite everything, Sylvia smiled. "Okay, but you think we should cool off. Hand victory to my mum and your boss?"

"No. Just till the end of your course."

"Three years," she whispered.

He nodded sadly. "A trial separation almost before we've started. But after three years your mum wouldn't doubt my intentions, surely. And it'll be nothing to do with the university any more."

"I thought the deal would be something like that. The just-good-friends routine for three years."

"Sounds like you've already prepared yourself. But what do you think about it?" Derek asked.

Sylvia hesitated. "I think it's a horrible idea. But I agree to it." She surprised herself with the resolve with which she said it. Deep down, she felt devastated but she could not deny the common sense. After all, she told herself, I'm not losing him. It's a postponement, not a cancellation. The only problem will be keeping my hands off him till the end of the course.

"They're not going to beat us, Sylvia," he said

defiantly. "Not in the end. I can't say I like what we've decided but we've been trapped in a corner by . . . events."

"Trapped in separate corners," Sylvia commented.

"Yes. I guess so," Derek replied. He looked at her and smiled reassuringly. "If it wasn't so corny," he said, "I'd say that absence will make the heart grow fonder. Yes?"

"Abstinence rather than absence, Derek."

He put up his hands. "Okay. But you've got to promise to try to behave, just as I have."

"I'll try to keep my mind on how good it'll be in three years' time to get my hands on you again. Possibly," she grinned, "during the degree ceremony."

"That might be frowned on, too."

"I won't care then."

Derek laughed. "Let's finish up and at least enjoy this afternoon. The embargo doesn't start till 16.17, when your train pulls out of Exeter."

"But it's not easy to make the most of it, knowing what's coming."

"It'll be easier when we've got used to the idea. When you've got stuck into work, industrial training, and I get stuck into more exam scripts, lectures and the rest of it."

"I hope so," she said.

Derek waved to get the attention of the waitress. "Come on," he said to Sylvia. "Let's get out of here and have a walk. Look around the shops, then to the green fields. Besides," he added, "I feel like buying you something. Yes?"

Sylvia just smiled in reply. She didn't want to say "yes" because she knew that it was a memento that he'd got in mind and she wished that she didn't need one.

Despite being a Saturday, the main street was not too crowded. The rain must have deterred the crowds. "Let's see," he said to her. "Something practical rather than sentimental, you say. How about a copy of Rose and Johnstone's mass spectrometry book? It'll be the first book you'll need when you get back to university."

"Nothing quite that practical! Besides, I won't need a boring book to read, I'll learn all about mass spectrometry at the forensic labs," she said. "No, maybe a Rolls or an imitation fur coat – though someone might think it's real. Let's see. What else?"

"How about that?"

They had stopped by the worst sort of souvenir shop. Cheap patterned plates, plastic doll and scent sets, the inevitable clotted cream, and paintings of dogs and children with enormous soggy eyes. Derek was pointing to a mug embossed with an incredibly ugly gnome and the words, "I am the world's greatest lover."

"Okay," she laughed. "I'll treasure it."

"Let's not get carried away before I check if I've got enough money on me."

When Derek came out of the shop, Sylvia was watching the mid-afternoon news through the window of the TV shop next door.

"Look," she said. "CAR at it again." Even without hearing the commentary, it was clear that CAR members had broken into some research laboratory and had videotaped the monkeys and dogs that would be used in experiments. The BBC was showing some of the amateur film. What struck Sylvia more than the sad-eyed caged animals were the masked protesters rushing down the corridors. Why the masks? Woollen, with just three holes for eyes and mouth. They looked just like terrorists.

Derek was shaking his head slowly. "They'll lose public sympathy. People in this country tend not to support even a good cause if extremists are behind it. You know, there are a couple of organizations that beaver away quietly behind the scenes, trying to find alternatives to animal experiments. The mood *is* changing, but the need for animals doesn't go away simply because CAR points out that they're used. No, the only way to change it is to find alternative tests. That's what the groups I've got in mind are doing – then nudging companies into accepting the more palatable alternatives. I haven't seen anything constructive like that from

CAR." They turned away from the window, Sylvia in silent agreement.

"You know," Derek said, taking her hand again, "I was once a bit of a rebel myself – went on lots of peace marches when I was your age. When it became clear that we weren't getting anywhere, some amongst us got angry – like those CAR people. Me too."

"Oh? What did you do? I can't imagine you doing anything . . . criminal."

Derek smiled. "I'm not the person I used to be. I threw a tin of red paint over an army barracks."

"Disgraceful! Did you get caught?"

"No. Too much of a crowd to disappear into. But I tell you, it doesn't do any good. It only gives a good cause a bad name – and it only made me feel guilty."

A little further down the street, Sylvia said to him, "When we were at Mark's, you said you thought the balance of terror approach to peace was wrong. You didn't say why."

"There's something awry when more and more weapons equates with greater safety." He paused. "It's like two cowboys facing each other in a street. The deterrent argument tells us that as long as they each have the same number of bullets neither will shoot. But we know it doesn't work quite like that. The act of posturing there in the street leads to bravado and then to foolhardiness. One begins to think that he's faster than the other or can catch him off-guard – that he can draw first."

"And you think the same about chemical weapons?"

"Yes. Only worse in some ways. Because they can be deployed furtively – which means they're more likely to be used. You can't deploy a nuclear weapon furtively. There's no disguising a nuclear warhead coming at you! Chemical weapons don't have the same macho image – perhaps that's why they don't get the same publicity. Anyway, remember they're dirt cheap and easy to produce as well. They're less reliant on heavy technology – virtually any country can make a chemical weapon of some sort."

"Yes. It's frightening. And sad. Such a perverse use of chemistry." She frowned. "Anyway, what's our next move, Derek?"

"How do you mean?"

"Crookland Bay Research Station. We've come to a dead-end, haven't we?"

Derek thought for a moment. "I wish I had a clear idea of where to go from here. I'll write to a few chemistry journals and try to get something of an anti-CBW bandwagon moving, I guess. If all chemists refused to work on chemical weapons, that'd be the end of it."

"No immediate solutions, then."

"Not unless you can think of one," Derek replied.

"No. Perhaps Mark . . ."

"That's what I'm scared of. He might . . . over-react. Do something dangerous. Keep your eye on him, Sylvia. Just in case."

"Yes," she said. "You might be right." Actually, she knew Derek was right. Mark would not just give up. He'd be planning something. Hopefully, she thought, he wouldn't get himself into trouble.

It began to rain harder. "Come on," Sylvia said, pulling Derek's arm and trying to shake off the depression his words had imparted, "Let's run!"

Derek grinned. "Huh. No contest." They set off at a trot. The rain got heavier and heavier. Cars sprayed them as they ran madly past all the sensible people huddled in shop doorways. Sylvia looked at Derek and laughed. His shirt and trousers were sticking to his skin and his hair was saturated. She noticed for the first time that it was getting a bit thin on top. She felt her own hair. The black curls that fell thickly to her shoulders were now flattened against her head and sent drips down her neck. The trickling was distinctly uncomfortable. "Where are we running to any-way?" Derek asked.

She stopped. "Somewhere dry. There, for in-stance." She pointed to a small cafe. "It'll do, won't it?"

"Anywhere will do."

They gave up the idea of a walk in the countryside and instead whiled away the time drinking coffee in a quiet corner of the cafe.

"All the good weather came in April this year," Derek said. "The showers were postponed till the first weekend in May."

"So it seems," she replied. "It's a good time for postponing things for the moment, wouldn't you say?" Her eyebrows rose significantly.

The train weaved its way along the coast, round and through the cliffs. Out of season and in the rain, the dreary little resorts were pathetic. Stalls were closed down, beach bungalows deserted, devoid of life. They were sleeping, waiting for sun and season to wake them. Then they would come alive with tourists in swimming costumes and Kiss-Me-Quick hats, ice-cream vans, kids with beach-balls, family games of cricket on the sand. She had always preferred the area in its sleepy state but now she saw things differently. How sad to spend half a lifetime just waiting for something to happen.

The train reached Crookland Bay five minutes early but, for no apparent reason, waited outside the station till it was five minutes late before it rolled up to the platform to let its frustrated passengers alight.

Chapter 24

It was lunchtime on Sunday when Sergeant Tims reported in person to Charles. "You were right, sir," the Sergeant said. "I've just seen the forensic report. Mark Little's prints matched those on the door knobs at Tedder's house."

"And in the bedroom where Tedder was found?"

"Yes. On the desk and the diary."

"Thank you, Sergeant," Charles sighed. "Get me a recent photograph of Little, will you? For press and TV release."

"The boys have got one. They're using it to trace his movements."

"Fine. Get me a copy. What have we got on him?"

"He took Friday's overnight Aberdeen train

from Broxton. He could have easily walked or hitched to the station. Anyway, he only went as far as Bristol. They haven't picked up a fresh trail there yet."

Charles nodded. "Okay. Keep me informed. And me only." The Sergeant turned and left, a little too military in style for Charles' liking.

He picked up the telephone and dialled as soon as the door closed behind Tims. "Hello," he said. "George? It's Charles here."

"News, is it?"

"Yes. All of a sudden, I believe in your chemist's intuition."

"You mean you've proved that Tedder had our T42?"

"No. That I haven't proved. But it's extremely likely. Mark Little was in Paul Tedder's house. Almost certainly on the night Tedder died. And now he's taken flight in the middle of Friday night. Heading north."

"Where, Charles? We must know where."

"We're working on it. He was last seen in Bristol. Have you got any ideas?"

"I can't say I have. I'll let you know if anything occurs to me."

"You'll hear from him soon, anyway."

"What makes you say that?"

Charles told him about a message he'd received that morning from London. Apparently a responsible newspaper editor had called the police over a story that he had been offered concerning Crookland Bay Research Station and, possibly, some missing chemical warfare agent. The editor was convinced that the caller was genuine. "Actually, George, the editor surmised that it was one of your own staff trying to leak information. A reasonable deduction under the circumstances."

"Was it definitely Little?"

"He used another name – Wrightson. But it looks clear enough. Tedder took the T42. Little removed it for his own purposes. I think his next move will be to contact you."

"You mean to bribe us with it?"

"A policeman's intuition this time. Yes, something like that."

"Have you searched his house?"

"We've had a good look round. Not a full search yet. But he'd be a fool to leave it there – and that he's not. He'd know that we'd find it. He'll have it with him if he wants to hold you to ransom with it." Charles went on, "My other main concern is over Sylvia Cooper. Her actions are clear now because she knew how Tedder really died – either because Little told her or because she went with him. We'll have to pull her in, George."

"She hasn't disappeared as well?"

"No. She's at home."

"Then why don't I have a word with her instead?

Tomorrow, after she reports for work."

Charles considered it. He didn't know enough about her to decide if heavy-handed treatment at the police station would open her up or close her down. He could always pull her in afterwards. "Okay, George. But don't push her in at the deep end. Find out if she knows that Mark Little's gone. If she doesn't, she's probably clean anyway. Then go on to the events of the night Tedder killed himself."

"Is that my first lesson in police interrogation?"

"No. You'll have a talk. We'll interrogate if we need to go that far."

"Okay. I'll be able to see her late in the morning."

"Right. Let me know how it goes because afterwards there's another decision to be made. What to do about Derek Thorn."

"Oh?"

"Let me tell you what Miss Cooper did yesterday. It may add bite to your persuasive powers when you're trying to prise information from her, because I doubt if she's proud of her . . . fraternization with Thorn. She'll know exactly what his role's been, and *she'll* be a less tough nut to crack."

Chapter 25

Monday morning. He was still dealing with the morning's pile of mail when the telephone rang. He recognized Dr Richards' authoritative voice straight away. "Dr Thorn," it said, "I don't have the time to put this in any way but bluntly, I'm afraid. Let me read word for word a note I received this morning. 'Dr Richards. I got your name from Paul Tedder's diary. But there was more than a diary. There was a suicide note and a vial. I think you know what is in the vial. I took both the note and the vial from Tedder's house. To show that I am no crank, I include the suicide note with this letter. The vial will not be returned so easily. There are two conditions attached. First, you must stop work on T42 and destroy all stocks. Secondly, as I understand it, you do research on chemical warfare because international law allows countries to retaliate against chemical attack with a chemical attack. You must renounce this right and in the current international talks, you must call for all countries to do the same. I was going to demand that you release to the press full details of your work and the true fashion in which Tedder, the CAR members and Mr and Mrs Banks died but I won't rub salt in your wounds. My aims will be met when you agree to the first two conditions and you can still save face. Think about my demands and have an answer ready for me when I contact you again towards the end of the week. I would not want to have to advertise your business to the public by opening the vial. But I would if necessary.' The note isn't signed but we both know who sent it. I'd say it was someone who's been talking to a chemist who knows quite a lot about CBW. What do you think?''

Derek found himself hot and sweating. So Mark had gone back to the house and taken the T42 after all. The thought appalled him. An infected dog could spend days in the sea and still pass on its fatal, man-made disease. What could a sizeable amount of the organism itself do? It was beyond imagination. But what concerned Derek most was the fact that the vial was in Mark's hands – a lad whom he had judged to be free of inhibitions and rather brash. A boy with a point to make and now with enough of a lethal substance to make it in the most dramatic way conceivable. He must be stopped – not because of what he was trying to do but because of the way he was going about it. For the moment though, Derek had to contend with Richards' insinuation that he was party to Mark's methods. He responded by saying, "Sylvia and Mark told me about the vial but as far as I knew, it remained in the house. I thought it was safely back with you."

"They didn't tell you that they'd taken it?"

"Let's get one thing clear, Dr Richards. Sylvia is not in on this. When she left Tedder's house with Mark Little, the vial stayed behind. In fact, she persuaded Mark to leave it after he'd suggested that they take it."

"Yes, I can believe that, because you and Miss Cooper no doubt share your secrets – and a responsible adult like you would not get mixed up in a crazy scheme like this. Right?"

"I just deplore that you have made it possible to put too heavy a weight on one pair of young shoulders." Derek shuffled the receiver to his other ear. "I want Sylvia Cooper left out of this. I can tell you all she knows – she knows nothing, apart from what I've just said."

"Yes, well, I'd have been seeing Miss Cooper

right now," said Dr Richards, "if it hadn't been for this letter from her boyfriend, a call to the police and now to you. But if you assure me . . ."

"I assure you. And," Derek added, "she is not his girlfriend either."

"But she once was?"

"Yes. What are you getting at?"

"I am trying to determine her loyalties – yours and Little's too. It's no great secret that you . . . how shall I put it? . . . liaise with Miss Cooper."

"What do you mean?" Derek asked, knowing precisely what Richards meant.

"Our policemen friends have been keeping an eye on Sylvia Cooper, and hence you."

Derek grunted contemptuously. "So why didn't you keep an eye on Mark Little too?" he snapped.

"They did, and he eluded it."

"Well, where is he now? What was the postmark on the letter?"

"Leicester. On Friday night he walked to a nearby station and caught a train to Bristol. There, the police found out last night, he switched to a coach as far as Leicester. He posted the letter there, in time for the noon post on Saturday. His further travels are not yet known, but he won't stay in Leicester. Let me try out a little idea on you." Richards coughed before continuing. "First, he'd probably opt for a big city to get lost in. That makes his puerile threats with the T42 more . . .

effective. The postmark and the police tell us he's in the Midlands – certainly a high population density. Maybe Birmingham – or Coventry. Why do I say Coventry? I'm not for a moment suggesting that you're aiding and abetting. I'm no psychologist but, if the possibility of killing is in his mind, he might leave his girlfriend well out of it down here, and take the opportunity to drag down with him the man who stole her from him."

Dr Richards had finished. The only sound Derek heard was a buzzing in his ear. He found it hard to speak. Dr Richards' reasoning rang true. Mark's infatuation with Sylvia was sufficiently strong that last year he'd thrown away his "A" levels because of it. Ironically, as a result, he had lost her. So this year he also felt bitter, against himself and especially against Derek. With such emotions, who knows what he would be capable of.

"Dr Thorn?"

"Yes," he replied into the telephone. "I'm still here."

"I'm sure you realize what a dangerous game he's playing, Dr Thorn. Dangerous for us all." Richards' tone had changed considerably. It was less official, bristling with insincere friendliness. Clearly trying to curry favour, Derek thought. "But I suggest that we can make it less dangerous if we send Sylvia Cooper up to stay with you and make sure he knows she's in the vicinity."

"No! You're too used to treating everyone as pawns, Richards."

Richards sighed. "Okay. You won't have that, but you must help us flush out this misguided do-gooder. Before he kills thousands."

Derek thought for a moment. His natural inclination was to help Mark, not Richards. All his sympathies lay with Mark, not the MoD. Yet Derek could not support Mark's method. It was too dangerous. The only cause that Derek *would* support was to make the area safe again. For everyone's sake. "I'll help," Derek said. "But let's make it clear, it's not out of support for you or your work. There's another thing as well," he added. "A condition. You must guarantee that Sylvia Cooper is left out of it. That means in the short term that she stays down in Crookland Bay and you forget about your interview with her. In the longer term, if anything happens to Mark Little and me, you must ensure that she is not . . . sacrificed in any way for the sake of covering up."

"Sacrificed? A bit strong, isn't it?"

"I would ask my sister about that but I can't."

"All right. Point taken. I'll do my best to protect Miss Cooper from the police and the MoD if you are absolutely certain that she has nothing to do with Little's actions. The police are already watching her. They'll make sure she doesn't leave the area. In return, I suggest you take a week or so off your teaching duties. Your Head of Department will not object."

"I'm sure he won't," Derek interrupted. "I gather you have a certain persuasive manner with Ian."

"He's a sensible man, your Head of Department."

As Richards talked, Derek could hear him rustling paper, probably in agitation. Derek frowned when he realized that with his right hand he was doing much the same – tapping his biro on the pile of mail. He forced himself to put the pen down. "I am right," he said, "in thinking that you have something specific in mind for this week or so – and for me, yes?"

"Indeed. Contingency plans. We must have some way of dealing with T42 up there. I'm sending you a couple of men to supervise the conversion of one of your labs at the university. They'll start first thing in the morning. They will also train you in the handling of T42."

"You do have a specific plan. What is it?"

"We all have our roles. The police will track him down. I'll string him along till they do. When they find him, we think it's best that he deals with someone he knows. We expect that it will be into your hands that the vial is delivered. We want you to have the facilities at your disposal and the knowledge to deal with it properly."

"Anyone can handle it if it's still in the vial. Mark Little's proved that."

"True, but we must have contingency plans. When you get it, we want you to render it safe. You can, once we've converted your ordinary laboratory into a specialized one. Certain new equipment you'll need and so on."

Derek did not pursue the matter. If Richards did have further plans he was not letting on. Derek was not sure if there was a real need to hold back at this stage or whether the man's life was so steeped in deceit and secrecy that it had simply become habit. "What if the police don't find him? What's your contingency for that?"

"Have faith in the police force, Dr Thorn. You'd be surprised how difficult it is to disappear if the whole country's looking for you. Especially when people believe that they'll be doing him a favour by revealing his whereabouts. Of course, in this case, they will be."

"You mean you've got yet another fiction to sell to the public?"

"In their best interests, yes. You'll no doubt see the news this evening – and the papers tomorrow."

Dr Richards actually seemed proud of his scheme, whatever it was. Derek tried to bring him down. "What if he carries out his threat?"

"Do you know the population of the Midlands? Evacuation is out of the question. Besides, it would be considered by Little as provocative, wouldn't you say? We must ensure that he doesn't have reason to carry out his threat."

"Like accede to his demands?"

"Come now, Dr Thorn. Be sensible."

"I am being sensible. Meeting at least some of his demands is the best way of removing the threat."

"We have considered it, as one of a number of options. Our only possibility is to engineer a mock cessation of our programme of research. Enough to convince a non-chemist. But it would be difficult even to mimic a close down of operations and yet maintain the safety of our . . . products."

"I wasn't talking about conning him," Derek replied in disgust. "I meant negotiate with him. Go some way towards his demands. Haven't you heard of negotiating?"

"Yes. I've heard of it, but this government does not negotiate with terrorists. And that is what Mark Little has become."

Derek continued sorting his mail, mechanically now. Company advertisements straight into the bin, lecture timetables up onto the board by his desk, letters into his in-tray. In other circumstances, two of them would have delighted him. One invitation to give a lecture in America, another to write a chapter in a chemistry book. But he had lost his appetite for small personal triumphs.

It was not long before Ian came with the news that Derek had been granted a short sabbatical period to concentrate on collaborative work with the Ministry of Defence. And no, Ian didn't mind if some alterations to the lab were necessary.

"Central Television. This is the six o'clock news as it affects your area." The piece on Mark followed the first item about the latest wage claim of workers at a car manufacturer. "The police are extremely anxious to trace this boy. He is staying somewhere in the area. It has been revealed in a medical check-up he underwent before leaving his home in Devon that he is seriously ill. So far the authorities have been unable to trace his whereabouts to make him aware of his condition. It is vitally important that he receives a course of treatment at the earliest possible opportunity. If you think you have seen him, ring this number or contact any police station."

The police had chosen a photograph that emphasized his thinness. It would be easy to imagine him suffering from some wasting disease. It struck Derek that they had not named the poor sufferer. Presumably, he thought, because they don't know if he's using his real name. It wouldn't fit with the story if the good citizen about to turn him in found he was using an alias. The good citizen might begin to wonder. And Richards would not be able to abide the public beginning to question.

*   *   *

Sylvia stared at the newspaper. She could hardly believe it. Mark's eyes were gazing at her, under the headline, "Have you seen this boy?" Something about a medical crisis. Something that did not fit Mark at all. And he was thought to be in the Midlands. Why there? Is it really Mark or has he a double? Don't be silly, of course it's Mark. You don't mistake someone who's been your boyfriend for four years. She was struck by a thought. The article had the same ring to it as the report of Paul Tedder's death. A convenient fiction. Had Mark done something foolhardy, knowing what he did about Crookland Bay Research Station? Was the MoD looking for him in their own imaginative way? It was Mark's nature to be foolhardy. She could well believe that he'd try something on. But what?

Her mum broke the spell. "You'll be late for work," she said.

Sylvia folded the paper. She did not want her mother to see it. Over breakfast, she couldn't face explanations – even if she had any. It would be bad enough this evening.

The picture of Mark plagued her all day long, like an annoyingly catchy tune that played on endlessly in her head. Eventually, she could stand it no longer. "Look," she said to Cheryl, "I really need to speak to my tutor. Is it all right if I use the phone in your office?"

"Yes. That's okay. Anything wrong?" Cheryl asked.

"Not really. Just a query over some course work."

She could remember Derek's home number. After the business with the lost camera, she couldn't forget it. But she had to use Directory Enquiries for the university number. Eventually she got through to him. He wasn't in his office but down in one of the labs. "I guess you know what I'm ringing about," she said.

"I can hazard a guess."

"It's about Mark."

"Yes."

"Yes. Do you know what's going on? It was in the paper this morning."

"I haven't seen a paper yet. It's all a bit hectic for me here at the moment but I confess that I know anyway. I'm afraid Mark's taken the law into his own hands."

As Derek outlined Mark's actions, Sylvia listened in amazement. Yet afterwards she did not understand her surprise. It was exactly what she would expect from Mark. It explained why he had not wanted to stay with her on the night they found Tedder. All the time he had been thinking of going back – after he had fooled her into believing that he'd given up on that idea. "What are we going to do about it?" she asked Derek.

"We? Nothing. The police are close behind him apparently. For better or for worse. There's nothing for us to do. I carry on lecturing, you carry on analysing forensic samples. Unless . . . Sylvia, has he ever been up *here* to visit you?"

"Yes. Near the beginning of the course. Why?"

"Did he stay overnight?"

"Oh, I see," she said. "Yes. Mitchell James had a spare room at his digs."

"I think the police would find that interesting."

The notion of the police catching Mark filled her with alarm but she wasn't sure why. Mark deserved to get caught. In a way. His dedication to a good cause, she couldn't fault. But his protest was too extreme. Just like the CAR members that had so repulsed her as she stood outside the television shop in Exeter. Did she wish that their actions had been prevented? Yes. To stop them damaging a good cause. She wasn't so sure about Mark, even though he was far more dangerous. She knew now that she felt no lingering love for him, so why the qualms? Because it was just conceivable that Mark's daring scheme might work. He might just succeed where Derek's reasoning had failed. She really wished that it could, but something told her that in real life such audacity would not pay off. Maybe her disquiet had a simpler cause. A fear of what Mark might do when confronted with the police. "You're not going to tell them, are you?" she asked, the trepidation clear in her voice.

"No chance," Derek replied. "I might act on it myself. But the police will trace him anyway, you know, sooner or later."

"What'll happen to him when they catch him?"

"That I don't know. Unquestionably his motives are good – not selfish at all. I hope it doesn't go too badly for him."

"Do you think he'd really let the T42 loose?"

"Surely not. He wouldn't be so callous."

I just hope you're right, Sylvia said to herself. At the other end of the line there was a sudden bout of hammering in the background. "What are you doing up there?" she queried. "Destroying the labs?"

"The opposite actually. Building one. And I'm supposed to be helping out."

"That's a hint, right?"

"'Fraid so. I'd better get on with it." He paused before adding, "Given Saturday's decision, I can't really say that I'm missing you, can I?"

Sylvia smiled contentedly to herself. "No. And I can't say it either."

The first thing to happen was the screwing of a notice on the door. DO NOT ENTER. MICRO-BIOLOGICAL HAZARD. Despite the fact that the laboratory chosen was not one that undergraduates had occasion to go near, a big black bug, comically drawn in indelible felt-tip, soon appeared under the warning plate. Some members of staff wandered into the laboratory to see how it was being modified but they were not made to feel welcome by the two MoD supervisors. The only member of staff that the technicians were instructed to tolerate was Dr Thorn. His were the only questions they were prepared to answer. And by no means all of them. He only had to know what was essential if he ever needed to use the lab for handling T42 safely. When all the old units had been hurriedly removed to leave an empty shell of a laboratory and constructive work began, a new lock appeared on the door. There were only two keys. The MoD workers had one, the other they gave to Dr Thorn. The university's own technicians were no longer required or permitted to help and academic staff were not allowed to enter. The two Crookland Bay men worked around the clock and over the weekend on their own.

Basically, they were erecting a laboratory within a laboratory, like a sleeping compartment within a tent. The outer part was some form of control room for the inner. It was the internal lab that took most care and attention. It could be sealed entirely from the outside world in case of accidents. Even the ventilation duct incorporated a shut-off valve. Leading to the centre of its roof, there was also a smaller pipe, clearly designed for pumping liquids. When Dr Thorn queried if the pump had been installed the wrong way round, one of the workers told him tersely that they knew their jobs well enough. The pipe was intended for delivering liquids to the lab, not for carrying them away. No further information was necessary.

Chapter 26

"If those corny detective films are anything to go by, you'll be tracing this call. I can't stop you, but don't send in the police. At the first whiff of the cops, I'll throw the vial. It's in my hand right now."

"If I may say so, that sounds like something out of an old film itself. An old-fashioned bluff."

"But you can't take a chance, can you?"

"Just a moment. I'll give an appropriate instruction."

"Hello?"

"Yes, Mr Little. Or should I say Mr Wrightson?"

"I didn't expect my identity or location to be secret for long."

"No. You're very astute, Mark. With your intelligence, I don't know why you're taking this course of action. It would be better for all concerned if you returned and came to see me . . ."

"I don't trust you, Dr Richards. And I'm clever enough to know that I've got you over a barrel. You can't trick me with your . . . coolness."

"I'm concerned about the danger you're causing – from the point of view of an accident. You are untrained and in possession of a lethal substance. But you're bluffing about releasing it deliberately. Do you know how many are at risk?"

"I don't want to know, and I'm not bluffing. So put an end to it, Dr Richards, or you'll see how serious I am."

"I can see that you're a hard man to dissuade. We will have to see what we can do for you. I find this phone most restrictive. We must talk about it face to face."

"No. That won't be necessary. I can verify whether you've carried out my demands from here. I'm keeping an eye on the scientific press who will report on developments at the disarmament talks. And a friend of mine who works at the Forensic Labs in Crookland Bay can check over your research station."

"Miss Cooper?"

"Yes. She can verify that the research has stopped, and stockpiles must be destroyed in her presence.

Then she can inform me and I will return this vial, also for destruction."

"That may be possible. But we'll need time. Such arrangements cannot be achieved overnight. Just let me check on one or two things. Hold the line."

"I'm not stupid, Dr Richards. You check over the next day or two. I'll call back."

Click.

When she returned with the file, Derek jotted down the address where the student lived. It was not one of the student residences but a house. He probably shared it with a few fellow students. Mitchell, like Sylvia, would be away for industrial training but Derek resolved to go there anyway. If Mark was using the same house again, it would be better for him to be discovered by Derek than by the police. Who knows what Mark might do if he felt threatened by officialdom. Derek was so uneasy about Mark's reaction to being cornered by the police that he did not tell Richards that he had a lead on Mark's whereabouts.

On the way back to his own office, Derek called in at the new lab. It was finished. He stood in the doorway of the inner room, startled by its cleanliness and its emptiness. Thirty square feet of whiteness. No windows, one door. It looked like a padded cell. A few electric cables poked into the room, their bare wires dangling, like worms coming out of the walls, waiting. No doubt the MoD men would bring in the equipment later. There would need to be a sealed cabinet in which the T42 could be handled, of course. In other circumstances he would have enjoyed playing with remote robot hands for manipulating dangerous items behind a safety screen. But when it was for real, it lost its attraction. The door closed with a click and a hiss. It had an ominous air of finality about it. Sealed, like an Egyptian tomb. Nothing out, nothing in. God help the people who work in labs like this all the time, Derek thought.

It was the canteen table that jerked whenever someone at either end leaned on it. The same one at which Sylvia had first met Paul Tedder. She was staring absently at a charred lamb chop when a man Sylvia had not seen before leaned uncomfortably close to her and asked, "May I sit here?" He indicated the chair next to her. Sylvia smiled warily and nodded. There were plenty of empty places elsewhere. His tray held only a salad roll and a coffee but he shuffled its contents around a couple of times before seeming satisfied. He was older than Paul Tedder, possibly Derek's age but bearded and more wrinkly. When he had stopped rearranging his lunch, he introduced himself. His breath already smelled of coffee. "Roger Hanson," he said. "Call me Roger. And you, I believe, are Sylvia Cooper." He had twisted in his seat so that his whole body turned towards her and he looked straight into her face. His manner was not so much annoying as discomforting. He seemed friendly enough. Too friendly. "Yes," she said. "And I'll be marrying my boyfriend soon."

The man belched, then cleared his throat and excused himself. "I'm sorry," he said. "I'm giving you the wrong impression. You might say that I'm after your mind, not your body. I have a few questions for you." He took a bite out of his roll and a piece of tomato slithered out and fell onto his plate. A few drops of the juice clung to his beard like a blood stain. "A devil to eat, these salad-laden rolls."

"Are you a policeman?" Sylvia asked.

"No, but I do help out when people go missing."

"You want to know about Mark Little."

He swallowed another mouthful, a few crumbs also lodging in his beard. "Yes. I'm to build up a picture of him. Not a physical one you understand. One that might help decide his likely behaviour."

"So what are you?"

"I'm supposed to be an expert at judging character, that's all."

Sylvia said, "You're trying to find out if Mark would release . . ." She stopped herself, looked around and asked more quietly. "How much do you know about this?"

"As much as I need to. I'm a loyal and trusted servant." He smiled. "That is, after I'd signed the Official Secrets Act."

"So what can I tell you?"

"For a start, you're not really about to be married, are you?"

"What's that got to do with it?"

"Everything, Sylvia, everything. Mark Little was your boyfriend. How would he react to such news?"

Sylvia shrugged. "It's not true."

"Does he love you?"

"Who?"

"Mark Little, of course. Who else?"

Sylvia looked up at the man and found that he was still staring intently at her. She looked away and muttered, "Yes, I suppose he does. My mum says he does and mothers are never wrong, are they?"

"What about my other question? Might Mark be jealous of anyone else?"

She nodded. "He might be."

"Dr Thorn?"

Sylvia felt a pang of guilt. "Why ask," she said sharply, "if you know the answers already?"

"I want to hear from you, not from some dispassionate policeman."

"Policeman?"

"Sylvia, you can't expect the police not to conduct a few inquiries." He finished off his lunch and took a drink of coffee. "How do you find Mark, in your own words?"

Sylvia shrugged. "Like a lot of sixth-formers, I guess. Likes to have a girlfriend around, likes some excitement. A bit headstrong, even. But," she added quickly, "not callous. He's an ordinary, nice lad."

"Does he show any interest in the various peace movements?"

"Not especially. He's against war, of course."

"Gets emotional about the issues, does he?"

She hesitated before answering. "No more than a lot of others."

"You must give me honest answers, Sylvia." Roger wiped his beard but only succeeded in spreading out the stain. "Neither of us should feel that we have to protect him. He doesn't need protection."

"I know. But why don't you simply ask if I think he'll . . . release it?"

Roger smiled. "Because I know the answer you'll give and it's one I don't need to hear from you."

"So what would I say?"

"You'd say that he couldn't be so nasty as to carry out his threat."

"True."

"But under normal circumstances, Sylvia. That's how you know him. He's hardly that now. And he's been jilted by someone he loves. How do you think he'll react under those circumstances? Perhaps surrounded by police officers. He'll be angry, won't he? What do you think?"

Sylvia's head drooped. "Yes. He'd be angry. But he wouldn't do it. Surely?"

The man ignored her question. "What's *your* attitude to chemical warfare?" he asked.

"Well, I . . . I don't approve. In fact I agree with what Mark's trying to do."

"But not how he's doing it."

"That's right. It's a terrible weapon."

Roger put his hand on her shoulder. "I'm here only to judge character, not morals." He removed his hand and cleared his throat. "Tell me, what does Mark think of Derek Thorn?"

"He hardly knows him. I don't know. Derek's on his side – he knows that."

"On his side as far as warfare is concerned. But what about you?"

"Me?"

"Has Mark ever been jealous about activities you've undertaken that don't involve him? Is he angry if you go out alone, for example?"

"Not angry, no. He wasn't happy when I left for college."

"Does he bear a grudge about that?"

"Not against me."

"Against who, then?"

Sylvia kept her face away from him as she answered. "Himself, I guess. He just wishes he'd been able to leave school at the same time as me."

Roger nodded. "He failed some of his exams, didn't he? You're saying that he blames himself. Why?"

"He didn't really fail. Just didn't get the grades he needed to get into university. Because he concentrated more on me than on his revision."

"I see. He must like you a lot. Does he definitely realize that you're associating with Dr Thorn?"

Sylvia was getting annoyed by his constant probing. "He's not stupid," she answered tersely. Roger looked at her but said nothing, waiting for the silence to do his work for him. Sylvia soon yielded to it. "But he's not going to give me up, apparently. Again, Mum says so."

"Do you agree?"

"Yes," she said quietly. "He's a persistent lad."

Roger slapped the table. "Excellent!"

"Why?"

"Well, why do you think he's . . . taking on the MoD and police?"

"Isn't it obvious? Chemical warfare and all that."

"Partly, yes. But partly to please you, Sylvia. You said yourself that he hasn't given you up. He's trying to win you back by putting an end to . . . something you both disapprove of. Love's a potent driving force. As long as he believes there's a chance of getting back together with you, he won't do anything to harm himself. And that means he won't harm anyone else, however reckless and insecure he may be." Roger pushed his chair back, clearly preparing to end the interview.

Before he could stand up to leave, Sylvia asked, "You sound so definite. Can you be sure?"

Roger grinned. "I feel that I've a good profile of him from elsewhere and you've added some extra bits and pieces, but I don't deal with the definite. In your present job you could tell me precisely how much heroin a person has taken – it's easy with hindsight and scientific methods – but I use only professional judgement and a crystal ball to decide *beforehand* if that person is likely to turn to heroin." He shrugged then smiled broadly. "I'm as sure as I can be."

Sylvia returned his smile out of politeness. "I see."

"I must go," he said rising to his feet. "But let me tell why I've disclosed my finding to you when I'm under strict orders not to. Because it's important that you should know. If Mark gets in touch with you, it's crucial to let him see a bit of light at the end of the tunnel, do you see? Don't abandon him."

Sylvia nodded. "Yes. I see."

Division Street was a long road that ran North out of Coventry towards Bedworth. Living up to its name, it cut through many different communities, like a cross-section of society. An Italian restaurant nestled against a Chinese grocer. Further on, Chen's Hardware neighboured Singh's Provisions. Mitchell James lived in the block of houses sandwiched between an Indian clothier and an adult video shop. Derek let four black children, all holding hands, skip past before crossing the pavement from his car to the front door.

The young man who eventually answered the

door was almost certainly a student. Derek had learned to recognize students without quite knowing how. "Mitchell James," Derek queried, "this is where he lives, yes?"

"Yes. And no."

"Away on industrial training, isn't he?"

"That's right. What do you want?"

"Truth be told, I don't actually want to see Mitchell. I'm trying to find an acquaintance of his."

"Yes?" the young man prompted.

"Yes." Looking directly into the lad's face for any sign of recognition, Derek said, "Mark Little. That's who I need to see."

The student hesitated before answering, but it could have been a natural hesitation – a moment's thought to try to place a name. "Mark Little," he said, shaking his head. "It rings a vague bell but . . . no, I can't say I've heard of him."

"Are you sure? Have you had any callers for Mitchell who might be this lad? He's a sixth-former."

"Are you the police?"

Derek smiled and shook his head. "No, nothing like. I'm one of Mitchell's lecturers at the university. Dr Thorn."

"Oh. So why all this fuss about a school kid?"

"Haven't you seen the papers? It's a personal problem I need to see him about. And I know that he knows Mitchell. I thought he might come here."

"Ah, yes. That's why the name is familiar." The student turned away from Derek and coughed twice. "Yes, I remember the news now. Some disease he's got."

"Yes, something like that."

"Well, we'll keep our eyes open, I'm sure."

"He hasn't been here yet though?"

"No. You could come in and look around if you don't believe me."

Derek forced a laugh. "No. There's no need for that if you say he's not been here. But is there anyone else in the house who might have answered the door to him?"

"Come in and ask them, if you like."

In the back room there were three other lads, all reading or writing. And, Derek noticed, there were just four mugs of coffee. Nothing to suggest a fifth resident. The student who answered the door announced to his flat-mates, "This is a lecturer from the Chemistry Department. He's trying to trace that schoolboy who doesn't know he's suffering from some disease. He knows Mitchell, apparently."

Derek asked his questions again but was reassured that they hadn't seen Mark Little either. "He's been here before, actually. First term, I think. Stayed for a weekend. Do you remember it?"

The students were all shaking their heads. "No," the first one said. "We all go home at weekends, I'm afraid."

"Well," Derek replied, "if he does come here, please give him a message. Tell him that it's in his best interests to contact me – you'll know the university's phone number – and we'll try and sort something out together. Tell him that I think I can help. Yes?"

"Will do."

Derek was none the wiser as he left but at least he had opened up another avenue for Mark if he was secreted in the house.

Chapter 28

"Ah, I'm glad you phoned." The voice was entirely different this time. It was relaxed. It had lost that anxious edge. "The whole situation has changed markedly since we last spoke."

"Oh?"

"My chief security officer has always maintained that not a single drop of T42 could ever leave this establishment. Events have proved him correct."

"How do you mean?" Mark asked incredulously. "I have some of it here, now."

"I really don't know what you do have, Mark. But we have all the T42."

"You can't have, Richards. I have the vial and Paul Tedder's notes say the log book for T42 wouldn't balance."

"That's perfectly true. Or at least was true until yesterday. Paul Tedder may have been a little deranged but he wasn't entirely mad. He knew the dangers of letting T42 leave here. He fooled us all, Mark – except the security staff. He concealed some of it here on the premises, then claimed that his vial at home contained it. An effective trick that had us all worried for a time. Effective but safe."

"But . . ."

"Yes, Mark. The vial. You have the vial. But it is not T42. Maybe it's water." There was a hint of humour in his voice.

"It can't be. It's yellow for one thing."

"Oh? How yellow?"

"It looks like . . . pee."

The trace of humour became a chuckle. "Perhaps it is. In ancient times, you know, soldiers used to urinate on their victims to emphasize the humiliation. Perhaps Tedder has done much the same to us. Clever, with a sense of humour too. It could well be. On the other hand," Richards added, "it may not be so simple. I suppose we should still treat it carefully . . ."

"You're bluffing. It is T42."

"You are hard to persuade. Still, we were convinced too – until we found the missing amount. We've analysed it and we know that it's our sample. Every single little drop ever made is accounted for. All present and correct."

"That's easy to say but how can you prove it?"

"I don't have to. I no longer have an interest in your actions . . . Well, that's not quite true. I am concerned about what's in your vial. I guess that I still have some responsibility for its safe handling. But the main threat is over, Mark. You're not in any sort of bargaining position any more."

"So if I dropped the vial onto the floor right here and now?"

"I'd say 'Go ahead' except that it must be classed as an unknown and possibly dangerous substance, so I think you'd better not. For your own sake. Tedder played his clever little trick, made his protest very vividly. Yet we don't know if he planned a sting in the tail with this vial."

"You *are* bluffing."

"Believe what you like, Mark. It doesn't perturb me. I could make a suggestion, though."

"What?"

"Why don't you get the contents of the vial analysed? I doubt if you'll want to bring it down to us, so how about a public analyst? Do you know any chemists in Coventry? You are in Coventry, aren't you?"

"Yes, I am. I've been on this phone for too long again. You're tracing it. Anyway, there's Dr Thorn at the university, I suppose."

"Fine. Surely you can trust him. He could analyse it for you. I could telephone him – warn

229

him that you're on your way, if you like. He could have everything ready to handle a potentially poisonous material. What do you say?"

"I say you're bluffing."

Dr Richards sighed. "All the more reason to get it to Dr Thorn. He could tell you for sure."

"I've had enough. I'm leaving before the police arrive. I'll think about what you've said."

"Good idea, Mark. It's a pity that you won't . . . Mark?"

There was silence.

Chapter 29

"No! Not backwards. You want to pivot sideways now. It's just like hand movements, remember. You'd turn with the wrist, wouldn't you? So move your wrist on the control. Yes. Look what's happening. That's it. Too violent, but smooth motion will come with practice. Just remember, it's like darts, forget your arm – the key's in the wrist. Wrist and finger pressure. Right," the MoD technician said, "you've got the flask where you want it so now you need to release it. It'll be trickier than you think. The robot will knock the flask over unless the fingers unclench precisely and the arm is lifted upwards and away perfectly vertically. So release your finger pressure steadily. Not too slowly, not fast." At first the mechanical fingers unwrapped themselves from the flask unwillingly, like an old and shaky arthritic hand, then suddenly they jolted apart leaving the flask on its side at the bottom of the cabinet. Derek swore. "Never mind," the technician said. "Told you that would need some working on. You're doing all right, though. Let's take a break."

On the way out of the inner sanctum, as he had named it, Derek pointed to the video camera on the wall. "What's that for? And the microphone?"

"If you and Little get in here with the T42, we'll want to see what's happening. There's a speaker coming in too – in case we need to give instructions or advice from out there."

"Me *and* Mark Little?"

The technician shrugged. "The boss reckons he won't hand it over to you till he's in the lab, apparently. Doubts if he'll let the T42 out of his sight so, yes, it'll be the two of you if it goes according to plan."

"I think," Derek said, "I think it's time I had a talk with your boss."

In the event, it was Dr Richards who called first. "I have some developments to report," he said, "which should precipitate Mark Little's bringing the vial to you." The Director of the MoD research station explained how he had cast doubts in Mark's mind on the contents of the vial.

"That's a hell of a game you're playing, Richards. As dangerous as Mark Little's."

"It would be, yes, but I took the precaution of getting advice on Little's likely actions. A psychologist has listened to the recordings of Little's phone calls, looked at his letter and conducted careful interviews with his parents, teachers and . . . so on. His conclusion is that Little is opinionated, a little wayward, and insecure but not suicidal. And, of course, he can't harm anyone with the T42 without killing himself."

Derek sighed. "I just wish you'd consulted me first."

"Why should I?"

"Psychology is hardly an exact science. Even you used the phrase, 'his *likely* actions'. You don't know how he'll react. God help us all if your psychologist is wrong. God help you. And," he added, "if that wasn't enough, I may have found out where he's living."

"We know that already. His phone call this morning was long enough to trace – a plain clothes man followed him back to a house in Division Street. And we had a few phone calls in response to the press release. But it changes nothing. Do you expect the police or army to go in, guns blazing?"

"Of course not. I could talk to him."

"You've talked in the past. If there's talking to do, I want it done in the lab where accidents can be controlled. Let him come to you, Dr Thorn."

"I was going to call you today, you know. I wanted to remind you that Mark's just a kid. A bright kid with a will of his own. I wanted to ask you not to hurt him. But I can see it's too late – you've already decided to try and manipulate him too. You're as wayward as he is, Richards. And when your two wills clash . . . Yes, I'll expect him. I'll play your dangerous game – but only because I have no choice."

Derek put the phone down and leaned back in his chair. "Hell!" He closed his eyes. So Richards' psychologist had consulted Mark's parents, teachers and . . . That hesitation haunted Derek. It meant something. It meant . . . Derek opened his eyes. "Parents, teachers and friends." Specifically, Sylvia! Richards had stopped himself saying it, not wanting to admit to breaking his promise to keep her out of it. Derek picked up the phone again.

The tide was fully in. Sylvia sat, her back to the dunes, with her hands buried in sand. "So this is where it happened," she said aloud. The beach had been opened again. She could easily understand how a man and a woman in love should come here on a whim in the dead of night and fool around on the beach and in the water. She would have suggested the same to Derek if his sister had never been to this stretch of sand and if he were here this night. They could strip off and go for a moonlit swim. He would approve of that. Afterwards, if it were cold, he would hold her close till she burned. If it were warm, they would make love in the dunes. She stopped her dream with a cruel smile. "Come on," she told herself. "You don't even know if he can swim." Out to sea, she could just make out a couple of ships, both tankers. Nearer, the waves crashed onto the beach, obliterating any memories of Ellen, Jack and a dog. The light was beginning to fade, taking away the heat of the day. Without Derek to keep her warm, she rose and walked slowly away, her arms folded across her chest.

Back at home, Sylvia and her mother said little to each other. In recognition of their private thoughts being diametrically opposed, silence preserved the peace between them. Sylvia dragged herself out of her chair, not bothering to announce that she was going to call Derek.

"Hello, Derek. It's me."

"Oh, good. Thanks for calling me back."

"Back? You phoned earlier?"

"Yes. I spoke to your mum. I asked her to tell you I'd called . . . Oh, she didn't . . . I see."

Sylvia shrugged. "Never mind. That's my problem."

"Perhaps she just forgot."

"Maybe. But I doubt it. Anyway," she asked, "why did you call?"

"I wanted to know if you'd been visited by a psychologist. Asking about Mark, that is."

"Yes. That's what I was calling you about. Name of Roger Hanson or something. Not a pleasant experience, either. Not a pleasant chap. He saw me at work yesterday."

"I thought so. He asked you all about Mark, yes?"

"He seemed most interested in our non-existent love-life. And about my relationship with you. He seemed to think that Mark's strongest driving force was his . . . love for me, nothing to do with chemical and biological warfare."

"And what do you think?"

"I don't know. Really I don't. What about you?"

"I'm not so sure either. We have to hope that you're such . . . an object of desire for him that he won't do anything foolish to hurt himself. But," Derek said, "I'm not convinced: firstly that it'll turn his battle against chemical warfare into a battle solely against me, and secondly that in the heat of the moment, whenever it comes, he'll be thinking in those terms."

"Nor me." So, Sylvia thought, we both disagree with the psychologist – at least partly. That puts Derek, and everyone else, in peril. "Derek," she said, "I want to come up to Coventry. I want to be with you."

"No!" Derek's voice was stern. A tone that

Sylvia had only before heard directed at persistent talkers in lectures. "Remember our pact."

"Damn the pact, Derek. You know why I want to be in Coventry."

"No, Sylvia. I don't want my style cramped. I don't want to be worrying about you as well as Mark. I can handle him better on my own."

"Handle him? You? What do you mean?"

Sylvia heard him draw a deep breath before answering. "I'd better tell you what's going on. But first, promise me you won't come up here and . . . add to my burden."

"If I'm reduced to the level of a burden, no, I won't come."

Sylvia pushed her hair away from her face but her fingers froze, interlocked with hair, as she listened in horror. "So," she said when Derek had finished, "you're going to . . . disarm him in this laboratory? It stinks, Derek. The whole idea."

"It's all right. It's a very special lab. There's very little that can go wrong. I've performed much more difficult and dangerous experiments than this one."

He sounded convincing enough but Sylvia remembered what a good actor he could be when he wanted. On the other hand, she could do nothing to stop it so there seemed little point in denting his confidence, even if she could. "I know you have. But . . . just take care. I . . ." She pulled her fingers out of her hair. "I'm very happy with my personal tutor. I want him in good condition in three years' time."

"And so you shall. You just keep your mind on the job, then you'll have a good degree and me to celebrate it with you."

Mrs Cooper looked up at Sylvia as she came back into the lounge, as if expecting to have to defend herself against a verbal onslaught, but Sylvia had forgotten about the message her mum had failed to pass on to her. She turned on the television and sat down, bringing her knees up to her chest and wrapping her arms around them. She stared at the screen so that she did not have to see what was in her mind. She listened to the programme, whatever it was, so she did not have to hear her own thoughts.

On the way back from Bedworth, Mark had gone one stop beyond Mitchell James's house before realizing that he should have got off the bus. It hadn't been unfamiliarity with the area that had caused him to miss the stop but his brooding on Richards' words. As he walked back to the house, he hadn't even noticed the car that had stopped behind the bus, and the man who got out and walked behind him at a discreet distance. Inside the house, he went straight up to his room – Mitchell's room. He didn't even bother with lunch.

The evening found him sitting on the bed stroking a sore and swollen hand. An injury that he attributed to Richards. Mark's anger had boiled over as soon as he'd finished talking to Richards. He'd slammed down the phone, turned round and punched the door of the kiosk – hard. His knuckles were now red and throbbing. But he was glad that it was only a hand – he had very nearly thrown the vial against the door. Instead he'd released his frustration through the punch and resisted the temptation to squander his chief weapon on a whim. If the T42 had to be released, he would have to set things up properly. So that everyone would know exactly what he was doing and why. So that everyone knew exactly what was being released. Without proper organization, it would be easy for Richards to come up with another story about another natural, infectious outbreak. Mark put his head in his hands and muttered, "Bastard!" He was referring, of course, to Richards.

The punch had helped. His anger was diminished. But it was still here, only controlled now. Controlled enough to reason. For the first time since this whole thing began, Richards had managed to get himself into the driving seat. "By disowning the T42 – or whatever it is – he's called my bluff. If," he thought, "I was ever bluffing." Mark was annoyed because he found himself in a situation that he had never envisaged. He had not accounted for Richards simply refusing to bargain. There were now only two avenues open to him. He could carry out his threat to open the vial or he could do as Richards had suggested and get the contents identified by Dr Thorn. It seemed a straightforward choice. The first would end everything, one way or the other. The second was not final, might get him back into the driving seat if it was shown that the vial did contain T42, and did not preclude the eventual use of the first option. It only required him to trust Derek Thorn. Mark was sure Dr Thorn would tell him the truth about the vial's contents, but would there be any tricks? "How can there be if I don't let the vial out of my sight? I'll hand it over only once we're both in a laboratory – with no one else there – and stay during whatever tests he has to make. It can't go wrong." He raised his head and addressed the poster of John Lennon on the opposite wall, "Can it?"

By the time that Mark was ready for company only Nick, a social science student, was in the house. The other three had gone down to the pub. "Bad news, is it?" Nick queried.

Mark slumped into a chair. "You could say that. Look," he said, "I've never really told you the whole story of why I'm here and why you've had to shelter me. Just enough hints of it all to gain your sympathy. It's time I came clean."

It was a cool, clear and quiet night. Perfect for

the council workmen who, working from an un-marked van full of electronic equipment, were erecting a small shelter over the manhole cover across the road from the house.

"You mean," Nick asked after he had heard Mark out, "you've got this . . . T42 here? In the house?"

"Upstairs."

"I think I'll go to the pub and join the lads."

"That won't save you."

"Getting drunk will."

"You don't approve, then?"

Nick sucked in a deep breath before replying. "Yes and no. You're absolutely right to take a stand. You've got to fight a thing like that. But how? It's one hell of a gamble you're taking. You can't open that vial. You wouldn't."

"Not now, talking to you," Mark replied. "But sometimes . . ."

"Mark, you can't. You've got to take it to this Thorn chap. It's the only choice left. He seemed all right when he came to the house yesterday." Nick tried to ease the tension by adding, "The sort you could buy a used car from."

Mark smiled reluctantly. "Maybe."

"Come on. Let's both go to the pub. We both need it."

"Okay," Mark said. "But I'll have to go up and get it first. It goes where I go."

"Oh, great. Some evening this is going to be."

It seemed to take an age to make the connection and to elicit a response to the ringing. Derek was not sure if it was his impatience or that it really was taking a long time. When a voice did come on the line, Derek's face dropped. It was not Sylvia. "Hello," he said, "is Sylvia there, please?"

"Who is this?"

"Derek Thorn."

"Again? Well, I'm sorry but you've missed her again."

"When will she be back? Do you know?"

"No. I've no idea."

Derek heard another voice in the background and an angry exchange. There were a couple of bumps and clicks then Sylvia's voice said, "Hello, Derek. It's me."

"Oh. I guess I've just had my first altercation with your mum."

"'Fraid so."

"I'm sorry about that but I'm very pleased to get to speak to you. Look . . . er . . . Men are funny creatures, Sylvia. They don't like showing emotions. I don't know why not. Anyway, I just wanted to tell you that I love you. I don't think I told you before." The line seemed to go dead. "Sylvia?"

"No," she replied. "You didn't say so before –

not in so many words. But I do know. Just as much as you know that I'm crazy about you."

"I'm sorry I had to say it over the phone."

"Why are we having this conversation, Derek?"

"I felt lonely, that's all. And," he added, "because I have to tell you that Mark's bringing the T42 to me tomorrow morning."

Another pause.

"How do you know? Has he been in touch?"

"No. He hopes to surprise me, so I don't have time to lay any traps. I know all this because Richards has just told me. And he knows because of the wonders of modern surveillance equipment that's installed outside Mitchell James's house. They've just listened in to a long conversation between Mark and one of the students in the house."

"I see. You were right about the house, then."

"Yes. The police found out for themselves. Anyway, I can't pretend to you, Sylvia. There's a risk. I can't see things going wrong but it's always there. So I called to let you know that tomorrow, Wednesday's, the day. Mark's adventure will come to an end then, for better or for worse."

Sylvia's voice sounded unsteady, only just controlled. "Take care of him, Derek. And take care of yourself."

"I remember you saying that things always work out for the best."

"Did I? That was about something else, not this."

"I got the impression at the time that it was a general attitude."

"Maybe. But I'm not so sure now. I hope to God it's true."

"Quite. Anyway, you'll be hearing from me whatever happens."

"Let me know as soon as you can. I won't rest till I know. I wish I could give you a good luck hug."

"I wish I could receive it. Keep your fingers crossed instead," Derek said.

"I don't want to put the phone down. It allows you to go and get on with it. Whatever you have to do."

"I have to get a good night's sleep. At least in theory. Anyway, I'll be in touch and . . . Well, there's no need to repeat it. I just wish I had you here."

Sylvia's voice perked up for a moment. "That's it! Why don't you tell him that I'm staying with you? He doesn't know – he hasn't contacted me. Then he wouldn't release it."

"Remember, neither of us fully believed that argument. And it could have the opposite effect. If he heard that we were together, he might turn on me. And if he turns on me, he turns on us all."

"Yes, true. Well, I'd better let you get your good night's sleep."

"I'm not keen on hanging up either. It means I can begin to think about all the possibilities for tomorrow. And I'd rather not. But there we are. I'll do what I can for him. You know you can rely on that."

"Yes. Look after yourself too. Love you."

"Yes. Love you, too. Bye."

There seemed so much to do but there was no time to do it in. He was not totally conversant with the robot arm. Another day's practice would have made life a lot easier. He also needed to arrange matters at work, to get the MoD technician's final advice and instructions before Mark arrived. There was a letter to write too. To say things that could not be said by telephone. He returned to his desk and pulled a piece of paper towards him. The letter was crucial but Derek found it difficult to concentrate. The right words eluded him. Still, if she ever did receive it, she would know what he meant.

Chapter 30

On Tuesday night, George Richards was invited to Charles' office as soon as the Little tape arrived on the police chief's desk.

"So," George said when he'd heard it through, "it's happening. But who's that Little's talking to?"

"We don't know yet. One of his flatmates. We'll find out when it's all over. Whoever it is, he'll be another one to keep an eye on, along with Miss Cooper, when this business is finished."

George nodded. "We're near to containing it now."

"Containing what? The weapon or the knowledge of it?"

"Knowledge. And I think we can rely on Thorn to contain the weapon. He feels partly responsible and, I think, pangs of conscience. Just what we need." George smiled confidently, the smile of a man whose plans were all coming neatly to fruition.

"Look at that. Bloody frustrating, isn't it?"

It was Wednesday morning and the black-and-white video showed Mark Little coming down the short path from the house, opening the gate, then walking along the road towards the bus stop. Eventually the camera could no longer distinguish his disappearing back. The screen went black.

George agreed. "He could throw it or just drop it. Accident or design. We simply can't touch him."

Charles frowned. "No. And we've lost our picture too. Still, we'll have radio contact till he gets inside that lab of yours. Then we can pick up pictures again because I've had it rigged so that your video signal is transmitted here as well as to your two chaps on the spot." He sighed. "I'm sure everything will be fine," Charles continued. "Even so, I would feel easier about it if I were up there, supervising the whole operation directly. If only . . ."

"If only?" George prompted.

"If only there weren't so much merit in keeping one's distance."

Chapter 31

Just another Wednesday. Not a special day. He would not tidy up, not make any special arrangements. He would not listen to special goodbyes from Nick and the others. Why should he? This was not the end of the affair. He was only going to get the contents of the vial identified. That's all. Then he would continue his campaign against this horrible weapon. Or was it a chemical weapon at all? He sat on his bed, the vial in his hand. He held it up to the light. It was pale yellow. Maybe just a little cloudy. What a relief it would be if the liquid turned out to be something other than T42. Yet how cheated he would feel if he had run away with, protected and treasured a sample of Paul Tedder's urine. How disillusioned he would be if it turned out to be something other than T42. No weapon, no further negotiations, failure. He would be no better than Derek Thorn. And in addition he would look foolish in Sylvia's eyes. Was he really doing all this for her? No, of course not. He was doing it for the world. Yet he hoped for a beneficial side-effect – the gaining of Sylvia's admiration. He would show her that Dr Thorn did not have the answer to everything. Yet to do that, the vial must contain T42. The glass of the vial was thick and strong at the bottom but at the top a line had been scored around the narrowest part of the neck. Clearly, it was there to facilitate opening. The top could be knocked off quite easily, Mark guessed. If he ever dropped the vial, it was hardly likely to break if it landed on its bottom. But if the impact was anywhere near the top . . .

Despite the fact that it wasn't a special day, he glanced around his temporary bedroom as if for the last time. It had been a safe refuge and he had grown fond of it. Derek Thorn had nearly intruded upon it but that did not matter any more. The whole house had been faithful to him and he was reluctant to leave its protection. Since the TV and newspaper pieces on him, he'd stopped mostly within the house and, when he did go out, he'd grown used to turning his face away from gazers. From today, though, he didn't have to worry about being recognized. Once he arrived at the university, he was baring himself. After what Richards had said on the phone, there were bound to be men watching the university buildings for him. He would be followed afterwards. The remainder of the affair would be conducted in the open. That did not matter if he had the T42. No one could arrest him, jump on him suddenly. Not while he held the vial in his hand. All he needed to do today was to keep the vial.

At the bus stop, there were four ordinary people – five if one counted the baby clinging to its mother. None of them took any notice of Mark. They mistook him for someone ordinary too. While the bus headed for the city centre, a persistent drizzle set in. Mark got off the bus at the terminus and pulled up the collar of his jacket to prevent the rain falling down his neck. To get to the university, he had to walk between two cathedrals. The old ruins on his right, the new on his left. He felt incongruous, guilty even, as he passed between them. If he had been religious he imagined that he would have felt as if they were standing sentry for him, giving him their blessing. He'd have liked the reassurance of a guardian angel. He stopped for a moment to survey the university building which was directly in front of him as Nick had explained it. If there were MoD men about, they weren't at all obvious. He took a deep breath and continued. Despite the instructions also given by Nick, Mark had to ask the way to the Chemistry Department. For a second he stood outside the door marked "Chemistry Office" before knocking and entering. His heartbeat raced. It wasn't the pleasant thrill of prowling on forbidden beaches now, it was fear. Fear of failure.

There were two secretaries in the office. Both looked up with enquiring faces as he entered. He wasn't sure which one he should address. He plumped for the older of the two. "Hello. I'm here to see Dr Thorn."

It was the younger one who replied. "His office is room 910."

"I don't know where that is," Mark replied.

"Is Dr Thorn expecting you?"

"No."

"Hang on a moment. I'll phone and check if he's in his office."

Someone answered the phone almost immediately after the secretary dialled. "Derek," she said. "Carol here. You have a visitor in the office." She listened to his reply then said, "Okay, just a second." She turned to Mark and asked, "What name is it?"

"Mark Little."

The secretary passed on the information and waited for Derek Thorn's reply. "Yes. Fine," she answered, then put down the phone. "Dr Thorn will be along in a moment," she said to Mark.

"Won't you take a seat?" Both secretaries resumed the clatter of their typing.

Mark did not have long to wait – to compose himself – before Derek Thorn arrived. When the lecturer came into the office, Mark experienced several sensations at the same time. Hostility – this man had taken away his girlfriend. Trust – in his honest, professional judgement of the liquid in the vial. Distrust – he represented authority, probably disapproved of Mark's actions. And trepidation – soon, with Dr Thorn's help, he would know the answer.

"Mark," said Dr Thorn, walking towards him. "I . . . er . . . What brings you here?"

"Do you really want to talk about it here?" Mark asked.

"Okay. Come along to my office."

The walls of the corridors were lined with noticeboards, photographs of staff and scientific equipment, timetables and careers information. No one took particular notice of Mark and Dr Thorn as they strode down the corridors in silence. Good, Mark thought, I wasn't expected. Dr Thorn stopped by a door bearing his name, unlocked it and pushed it open for Mark.

"After you," Mark said. He was not going to take any risks at this stage. The office was unexceptional. Cluttered with papers, shelves, filing cabinets and posters on the walls.

"Take a seat," Dr Thorn invited.

"You take the chair nearest the door," Mark said. "In case anyone should burst in. I'll sit over there by the window."

Dr Thorn's eyebrows rose significantly. He was not used to the cloak and dagger business and seemed surprised by Mark's aptitude for it. "What can I do for you, Mark?" he asked.

"Before I go into that, has Richards or the police been in touch with you?"

"Yes."

"When?" Mark queried.

"When you disappeared. They were trying to establish complicity, or not."

"What?"

"Well, they'd seen you, me and Sylvia together. They had to check if I was involved in what you were doing."

"Did they check out Sylv too?"

"Not directly. I convinced them that you were . . . going it alone."

"Good," Mark replied, pleased to keep her out of it. "Have you heard from him since?"

"Who? Richards? Why should I? He knows that I had nothing to do with it. Besides, we do not see eye to eye, Richards and me. I dare say he does his best to avoid me."

Nick was right – Dr Thorn did have an honest face. He seemed to be on the level. And if he hadn't spoken with Richards recently they could not have worked out a plan to ensnare Mark. There could be no trap without this lecturer's co-operation. I'll proceed, Mark thought, but with care. Thorn might be a good actor. "Okay, then," Mark said. "I've no need to mess about with you. You know what I've done." Receiving a nod from the lecturer, Mark continued. "Dr Richards tells me that what I have in this vial is not T42." He pulled the flask out of his pocket and showed it to Derek Thorn, but did not put it down.

"What?"

In Dr Thorn's eyes, Mark read surprise and even fear at the sight of the vial. "He tells me all the T42 is safe. That Paul Tedder was kidding us. I think it's Richards who's kidding. What do you say?"

"What do you want me to say? On one hand, it would be very convenient for Richards if it wasn't T42 but would he really say it wasn't T42 if it is? Could he risk you throwing it away or something?"

"He might risk it if it forced me into coming here into a trap."

"Trap? And in what way were you forced here?"

"Richards said you could analyse it."

Dr Thorn hesitated. "Yes, I could, but it's not a job for me. I'm not a specialist in such toxic materials."

"Maybe it's not toxic."

"Maybe. But in chemistry we always treat unknowns as if they were the worst possible case. And so I naturally regard that as T42 until it's shown that it isn't."

"But you'll check it for me anyway."

Dr Thorn sighed. "Why don't you hand it over to me, Mark? End it now. Irrespective of what's in the vial. It'll go better for you in the end. You've done all you can. And I admire the stand you've taken – I really do. But you can't take on a man like Richards . . ."

"I can if this is T42," interrupted Mark.

"And if it is, you're putting thousands of people at risk, Mark. Give it to me. I'll return it safely to Crookland Bay and then we can talk about their work in a more civilized way. Please."

"You've talked in your way – with no result. Now we'll talk in my way – with this," he said, shaking the vial, "in my hand. Now, will you check it for me or not?"

A look of resignation came to Dr Thorn's stressed face. "Yes. I'll do it. We'll have to go to a special poisons lab a couple of floors down."

"Special?"

"You don't handle stuff like that in a test-tube on a bench, you know."

"Okay," Mark said. "Let's go and get it over with."

On his way out of the office, Dr Thorn donned

the white lab coat that hung on his door. Back in the corridor, a student walked past, greeted Dr Thorn, and asked in a cheeky voice, "Did you forget the lecture on Monday, then?"

The lecturer hesitated, as if he still had forgotten it. "Monday? No. How could I forget you, Mick? Sore throat, that's all. I'm arranging a two-hour stint for you next Monday to make up."

"I think *I'll* be ill then," the student retorted.

After he'd gone, Mark said, "Sore throat? You seem okay now."

"Not so bad, thanks. It only hurts now if I have to shout to a whole class."

"Mm."

"Nothing sinister in it, Mark. Lecturers are prone to that sort of thing. Come on," he said, "we'll go down the fire exit stairs. There's less people about."

"That won't matter," Mark replied, "if there's any tricks. It won't stop at one staircase."

Dr Thorn was clearly trying to keep an indignant expression from his face but he still looked sorely tried. "I know that as well as you, Mark." He stopped on a landing. "What I can't understand is that you might kill thousands of people but you still carry on. Be responsible, Mark. Do you really want lots of deaths like Ellen's? You can't be serious about releasing it."

"I can. To save millions in the future. That's what happened with the nuclear bomb, isn't it?

Hiroshima was just a show of strength which successfully put an end to a war."

"But did it stop the nuclear arms' race? Of course it didn't. It might even have accelerated it. You're trying to stop chemical and biological weapons but if you let people see what that stuff can do," he said pointing to Mark's pocket, "you could scare the opposition into developing it themselves. Would you be proud of that?"

Mark had not thought of it like that before. He was surprised. He'd had so long to think about it and how far he was prepared to go. At times he believed that he could break the vial to induce such abhorrence in the weapon that it would never again be used. Yet the fact that he would kill Nick and the other lads, the baby at the bus stop and . . . everyone, withheld his hand. If only there was some way of restricting it – just to give people a taste. But now, Derek Thorn was suggesting that it could have the opposite effect anyway. Things were not so black and white as Mark had hoped.

"Look," he said. "I know you're just trying to get this vial off me. You're probably on Richards' side. But I haven't come all this way to give up now. As long as it's T42," he took it in his hand once more, "I can bargain. Even if I wasn't prepared to throw it down these stairs, Richards doesn't know that. I intend to win by not having to release it."

"Win? How can you win? Richards has got it all sewn up, even if he accedes. Let's say he destroys all stocks. Stops all work on it. You still can't erase it from history. For better or for worse, it's with us now. It'll be on numerous records. It could be revived anytime. It's documented, Mark, and there's nothing you can do about that."

"But . . . I'd have taken a stand. I'd have slowed it up. That's worthwhile in itself. So let's get to that lab of yours!"

Dr Thorn groaned audibly then shrugged. He turned and led the way down the stone steps.

Damn him, thought Mark. He thinks he's so clever. The hostility he felt for Dr Thorn turned to hate. Mark's only comfort was derived from the fact that, if he really did let loose the T42, Sylvia's lover would get it first.

"This is it," Dr Thorn announced. He indicated the door that led into another corridor. "The lab's the first on the right. Are you sure, Mark?"

Mark looked through the window in the door. There were a few people milling about in the corridor and two men reading a notice-board just past what he took to be the door to the lab. Nothing suspicious. "Yes. You lead the way."

"Okay. Give me the vial."

"No chance."

"How am I going to analyse it, then?"

"With me right by your side. No tricks,

remember."

The lecturer opened the door and led the way to the laboratory. There was a notice on the door that Mark read as Derek Thorn fumbled for his key to the lab. "What's it mean, microbiological hazard?"

"It means that any work on infectious organisms is done in here. It's designed for it."

"Are these things common?"

Dr Thorn opened the door. "Come in," he said. "You first."

The chemist stepped inside. "No one else here," he said, indicating the empty room.

Mark entered gingerly, suspiciously. "You didn't answer my question."

"What things do you mean?"

"These special labs."

"They're not uncommon. Come on, we have to go in here." Dr Thorn opened the door to the inner laboratory but Mark was still looking at the outer room. "What's this bit for?" he asked.

"That's just for ordinary work. We need this inner part. Come and take a look. There's a cabinet with a robot arm for handling nasty materials."

Mark suddenly felt vulnerable. The whole set-up did not feel right. "Bit of a coincidence, isn't it? You having these facilities."

Derek shrugged. "Not really. As I said, they're not uncommon. Our biologists here work on all sorts of infectious diseases."

"That's what Richards calls his work."

"You keep putting me in Richards' camp, Mark. And I don't like it. I have – and want – nothing to do with him. Or you if it comes to that. Because I want nothing to do with chemical warfare. I'd sooner leave here right now. I don't relish the idea of working with that stuff, you know. It frightens me. The whole thing does. I'm on *your* side, but everything you've done frightens me. So if you're unhappy, let's leave right now."

Mark put up his hand. "No. Show me your lab."

Dr Thorn entered the inner room. "Look. Not much in here really. Here are the controls for the robot arm. We'll put the vial in through this hatch. It's sealed afterwards. Then I can do everything automatically from here. All I need is in the cabinet. Perfectly safe."

Mark looked in from the doorway. It was a small room. White. One chair, the sealed cabinet by which Dr Thorn stood, and a work bench stretching around two of the walls. On the bench there were two weighing devices of some sort and lots of bottles. The overwhelming impression was of cleanliness. "It doesn't look used. It's too clean – like an operating theatre."

"Exactly. Both this and an operating theatre need to be clean to stop disease spreading."

"I see," Mark said. "You say everything you need is in there already?" He nodded towards the cabinet.

"Yes."

"Convenient, isn't it?"

"Look, all I have to decide is whether that vial in your hands contains living tissue producing toxins. The test's the same whether it's typhoid bacteria or whatever. The chemicals I need are in here. Take a look for yourself."

"How did you know they were in there?"

Dr Thorn showed impatience for the first time. "Because they always are. They're never taken out."

"All right," Mark said. "But don't try anything."

"I'm hardly likely to, am I? Just come in and give me the vial. The sooner I get cracking, the sooner we'll know."

Mark stepped into the laboratory, still clutching the glass flask in his hand. Derek Thorn stepped to the side to let him pass. "What are you doing?" Mark snapped.

Dr Thorn put up his hands in a gesture of surrender. "I was just moving aside. I thought you'd want to move away from the door – as you did in my office."

"Just a minute." Mark looked around again. Above the door where he could not see it before, there was a camera mounted on the wall. "What's that?"

"A camera. It monitors the lab in case of accident."

"And if there *was* an accident in here?"

"How do you mean?"

"What action would be taken in case of an accident?"

"Oh, I see," the lecturer said. "You see that little box by the door . . . Here, let me show you."

Before Mark realized what was happening, Dr Thorn had edged past him and pulled the door shut with the small brass knob at its centre. It closed with a click and a hiss. Mark looked at Derek Thorn's face and knew. "You've . . ."

"I've simply closed the door. Just give me the vial and we can get on with it."

"You've done something! This *is* a trap." He pushed his way to the door and hit the knob but the door did not budge. He tried to pull it then turn it but the knob wouldn't move. He could not see how to open the door.

"No trick, Mark. It's a safety door, that's all – it won't open when the lab's ready."

"If it's not a trick, open the door," Mark shouted.

"But we're in here to do your analysis."

Mark raised the vial threateningly. "Open the door!"

"Steady, Mark. The door has to be closed for me to do the test. Don't you want to know what's in the vial?"

"I don't believe you," Mark cried. In frustration, he banged at the door with his fist. "This room seals in case of accident! You *are* working for Richards!"

"That's not true, Mark," Dr Thorn sighed. "But I had no choice. I had to protect the public. We're isolated in here. It's all over. You can't win. So give me the vial. Let's end it sensibly."

Trapped. Beaten. Mark had never felt such an anger. Against Thorn. Against Richards. Against himself. Deep down, he realized now, he had known that he was walking into a trap, but he thought he could play the game and win. Why hadn't he heeded his own misgivings? Because he had the T42. He thought it made him invincible. But Derek Thorn had tricked him. First Sylvia, now this.

Sylv. She's mine! This stupid lecturer hasn't known her all those years. He hasn't sneaked out after midnight to be with her on the dunes. He didn't help her through her GCSEs by quizzing her from revision notes. He didn't care enough to fail his "A" levels for her. He didn't give her her first taste of sex. I did.

A cold quiet night. Sylvia was in a teasing tight jumper. His hand slipped inside it. He could still remember the soft material of her bra and, through it, the surprising weight of her breasts. And since then she'd demonstrated lots of times that it was him that she loved. In his room when his parents were out. A couple of times on the dunes. She was terrific. Now, the memories only heightened his anguish. And his anger.

With Sylv and me, it's the real thing. Whatever Dr Derek Bloody Thorn's done to her, he's just . . . gratifying himself. Not Sylv. He doesn't know her like me. I'm not going to be beaten by someone like that. Someone after a quick lay with a girl half his age just to prove he's still got it. Not caring for Sylv herself at all. No, I'm not going to be beaten by him. I am invincible with the T42. Okay, so I can't win. Can't win her back. But I can't lose. And if I can't win her, neither will Thorn.

Mark's fingers tightened around the glass.

It all seemed to happen so slowly. A wildness developed in Mark's eyes. The muscles in his face grew taut with anger. His lips pursed with determination as he inhaled his last breath of clean air. His arm drew back and he threw the vial with all his might. It was so slow, Derek felt he should be able to dive across the room and catch it before it crashed into the plate glass of the cabinet. But he didn't move. He couldn't move. He was paralysed by shock. All he could do was utter a cry, "No!" But by then it was too late.

The vial splintered on impact, burst open, fragments of glass tinkled on the floor. The liquid seemed to hang there for a moment before splashing over the window of the cabinet, some bouncing from it, beading in the air and falling. The bulk of the liquid ran down the window and formed a small harmless-looking puddle on the floor. The globules left on the plate glass hesitated then, gathering momentum, raced each other down the pane. The rivulets streaked to the bottom of the window and caught on the sill. The liquid collected there at first. Then it ran along the lip and trickled to the floor, the drops plopping into the pool that had already collected below. Neither Derek nor Mark said a word. They simply stared at the mess on the floor.

Of all the possible outcomes Derek had considered, this one had been uppermost in his mind. In almost expecting it, he had prepared himself for it. He was resigned to the fact that, in a moment, a boy's rage could put an end to his life. Now, he felt more for that boy than himself. It seemed to Derek that Mark's last few weeks were like a whole youth, like his own, but telescoped in time. He wasn't so old that he couldn't remember what it was like. First the optimism. Peace marches and protest songs. Then the dreams faded with the realization that the powers-that-be didn't care – that they were immovable. There was little left but escapism. In that phase, several of his contemporaries had turned to drugs. But not Derek. He had embarked on an ineffective, harmless and short-lived anarchy that ended in pessimism and guilt.

When Mark had set out on his mission, he must have been fired by a great optimism. Doubt would have crept upon him when Richards started weaving his web. Wishful thinking – pure fantasy – would have kept him going, and brought him to Derek. He must have known it was all over, really. Then Mark too turned to anger. Derek *had* seen it coming. But Mark's short rebellion, unlike Derek's, was not confined to a tin of paint. The disillusionment that followed was total. Mark slumped to the floor, looking guilty, foolish, defeated. Spent.

There was the noise of someone clearing his throat and then a voice. "Can you hear me?"

"Yes. We can."

"Fine, no need to shout, just speak in your normal voice."

"Yes. Just normal. Everything's normal."

Mark looked up to Derek and asked, "Microphone and speaker?" Getting a nod from Derek, he said, "Those two men who were outside reading the poster?"

Derek nodded once more. "MoD men."

The voice sounded again. "I . . . er . . . I find this rather difficult."

"I can imagine," Derek replied sarcastically. "But you knew as well as I did that this was a possibility. I'll tell you what," he said, "*I'll* make it easier for *you*. Let me ask you a few things. Are we really isolated? Was the air vent off?"

"It was set to close as soon as the door shut. Everyone outside is safe. You're on your own air supply now."

"How long does it last?"

"Several days."

"How long do we last?" Mark asked, the bitterness clear in his tone.

The voice did not reply immediately. "You have several choices. I can tell you how to shut down the air supply. That's one possibility. Another is in the box by the door. You'll find two doses of something that will help."

Mark interrupted, "Painkillers, is it?"

"No. But they will provide a painless . . . end. But," the voice went on, "there's something you should know before deciding. In our initial testing with rabbits, one in five hundred had natural immunity to T42. Maybe it's the same for humans. We don't know. On the other hand, death by T42 is not pleasant."

Derek looked at Mark but Mark only shrugged. "What you're saying is that if we simply wait, there's a slight chance that we survive, yes?"

"Yes."

Derek pondered on it. "We could survive, but we could never leave here, right?"

"We're not sure. We don't have much option for decontamination procedures. We could try to protect you from the agents we must use to flush the lab but, yes, they may be fatal in themselves. There's a chance, though."

"What about those immune rabbits? Don't they hold the key? Haven't you learned anything from them?"

"No. You see, once our fundamental work is done, further work and development is carried out in the States. Their workers haven't yet found anything that distinguishes immune rabbits from ordinary ones. It's early days yet but they're working on it."

"Great," Mark snapped.

"We're sorry. But you must make the decision."

"How long before the T42 . . . kills?"

"In such close proximity, not long. An hour maybe."

Derek looked to Mark for his opinion but his expression told Derek that he no longer cared. Derek too sat down, propping his body against the door. "We wait," he said. "While there's a chance, we'll just sit here and wait."

"Funny, isn't it?" Mark said. "I was fighting for a cause so important that the lives of ordinary people – like you and me – faded into insignificance. Yet that *was* the cause – the lives of ordinary people like you and me!"

"Was that it, Mark? Really? Or is all this just a fight between *us* – over Sylvia?"

"Does it matter?" Mark looked up at Derek.

"No, it wasn't Sylv . . . Sylvia. But I think I threw it because of her. She loves you, doesn't she?"

Derek nodded. "Yes. It's taken me a while to realize it but, yes, she does."

"And you? Do you love her?"

"Yes. I didn't see that coming either. Not till Ellen . . . Not till this whole thing started. But now I know. Yes, I love her."

Mark looked away, an immense sadness in his eyes. Suddenly, Derek thought, Mark must have been struck by the uselessness of his action. Or was it that at all? Mark had known that it was all over with Sylvia. He simply wished to deny Derek the happiness of being with her. In that, he had met with total success. His despair had some other cause. Derek guessed Mark had just realized that, in deciding to break the vial, he had only thought of himself and his rival. He had not considered Sylvia at all. He was devastated now because he had condemned her too. He had denied happiness to the one who most deserved it. Derek wanted to console him, to tell him that he needn't feel guilty about it, but he could not. He had no right to forgive Mark. It was Sylvia he had wronged and it was Sylvia who would have to forgive him.

Still keeping his eyes averted from Derek, Mark said, "We were lovers too, you know, me and Sylv. For a long time." He paused as if reminiscing. "I can't remember Sylv ever being a *girl*. When all her school chums smelled of cheap scent and bubble-gum, and had bodies like . . . beachballs – beachballs with pigtails – Sylv was . . . well . . . a woman. You know."

"When did you first meet her?"

Mark gave a wry smile. "It was all very romantic between us. Childhood sweethearts, as they say. We didn't vow to marry in the school playground. Not quite. Not that corny. But it all got serious when we were fourteen, maybe just turned fifteen. She was . . . mature even then." Mark broke off, seeming to enter his own dream-world.

Derek watched him, this bright dying boy, and felt guilty himself. A little more willpower, more restraint, and he might not have provoked Mark into taking such a violent revenge. Derek might regret his involvement with Sylvia now, but he could not wish that it had never happened. He could not renounce the tranquillity and the magic of being with Sylvia, the euphoria of loving her. No. He was glad it had happened. But he regretted the outcome. Sitting on the floor of this God-forsaken lab watching the destruction of her young boyfriend. See how he scratches at his cheek and leg, Derek thought. It has begun to take effect.

Derek felt no resentment towards Mark. Most of the blame he placed on Richards. As he sat on the cold hard floor of a dreary, contaminated room,

Derek imagined Richards sitting in his plush office, well away from the incident that he had orchestrated. Derek could almost see the smile on his face. For Richards, the affair was all but finished. Most satisfactorily. The end could have been improved only if Sylvia had been by Derek's side. Then there would not have been even one loose end. Richards would be composing his next press release. Laboratory Accident at University: Two Dead. A neat story with no MoD connections. How Richards must be hoping that I don't have natural immunity, Derek thought.

"Derek," Mark asked, "why didn't they just gas us? Some knock-out gas?"

"Because you might have dropped, or thrown the vial as you fell. They didn't want to provoke you or cause an accident, not while there was a chance of retrieving it safely."

"I see." Mark tried to move his left leg but apparently could not. He scratched at it instead.

Derek went on, "I was meaning to ask you. If I'd tackled you on the stairs, tried to wrench the vial from you, would you have deliberately broken it then?"

Mark shrugged. "I might have dropped it anyway."

"Yes. That's why I didn't."

Mark's face grew more red by the minute. Small crimson veins showed in his cheeks where he had scratched them. "I was going to ask you something too. What was it?" He lifted his leg with both hands and moved it to a more comfortable position. "Oh, yes," he said, swallowing hard as if there was a nasty taste in his mouth. "How come you had all this ready for me? You knew I was coming, didn't you?"

Derek nodded. "The police found where you were living. They had some long-distance listening device on you last night."

"You didn't tell them where I was, did you?"

"No. Sylvia told me that you'd been to Mitchell James's house before so I checked it out. But the police traced your call to Richards and followed you home."

Mark grunted derisively, at himself or the police, Derek could not fathom. "Remember when you came to the house?" Mark said. "Nick coughed twice. That was a warning. I hid in a wardrobe in the bedroom. A bit like one of those stupid farces."

Derek smiled. "I thought it might be something like that."

Mark turned his head away from Derek and spat on the floor. "I feel terrible," he said. "Can't feel my left leg at all. Like it's been cut off but I can see it's still there. It feels heavy as well, when I lift it."

"Yes," Derek said. "I know. But I suggest we don't talk about it."

"Why not?"

"They," he replied glancing up at the camera, "will be watching. I don't want us to contribute to their knowledge about T42 more than we have to, just by dint of being here."

"You mean we're human guinea-pigs?"

"It's a golden opportunity, wouldn't you say? To study the effects on humans. I doubt if they'll let it pass."

Mark groaned, then coughed. "You said you admired what I did – tried to do. Did you mean it?"

"Sure. If I were your age, I'd have done something similar."

Age, Derek thought, and responsibility. That's the only difference between us. We both hate chemical weapons, we both love Sylvia. We just have different methods. Derek had yielded to pressure when he postponed his relationship with Sylvia. But Mark wouldn't yield to the pressure of Derek's intrusion into his love life. Mark *was* obstinate enough to say, "Sod this," and do something about it. It was much the same with his protest against the MoD and T42. "I admire your . . . resolve," Derek added, "but I also tried to warn you against it. 'Richards has got it all sewn up,' was supposed to be a hint. Not a good one, I'm afraid."

Mark was sick this time. He did not bother to

move even when the bile on the floor began to soak into his trousers.

"It was Winston Churchill who said that he didn't understand the squeamishness about the use of chemical warfare," Derek commented. "He wouldn't have said it if he was in here with us."

Mark began to look disinterested. A faraway expression crept into his face and his body swayed from side to side. Next time he was sick, there was blood in the vomit.

Derek wondered what hurt Mark more, the physical pain or the humiliation of being here. "There is one hope left, Mark."

"Oh." It wasn't a question, not a prompt for an explanation. It was simply an acknowledgment that he could still hear Derek's voice.

"Sylvia. She's our hope."

"Sylvia," Mark repeated. "I didn't even phone her. I thought they'd be listening in and I couldn't talk to her like that." His voice gurgled in his throat. "Haven't heard a word from her for ages. I should be with her. Not here."

"Yes," Derek said. "She'll be thinking of you now."

Mark was no longer acknowledging Derek's presence or words. He muttered, "My own fault really."

"What?" Derek asked quietly.

"That stupid 'A' level business. Losing her."

Mark wasn't answering Derek, he was just thinking aloud. "Shouldn't have got into such a brainless temper. About seeing her. If I'd made it to college as well . . ."

"Don't blame yourself, Mark . . ." Derek stopped denying the truth because Mark heard nothing anyway. His eyes were glazed. His face hot and red. "I've messed in my pants," he said, like a little boy confessing to his mother. "Sorry."

"It's all right," Derek replied. "It doesn't matter."

Derek tried to reason with himself but could not deny what his eyes seemed to see. The walls pulsated, tilting one way then the other. A little at first, then the whole room lurched and rolled. The cabinet was on his right one moment and on his left the next. Mark's convulsing body reeled before him. Sometimes it was horribly close, its vile smell pervading everything, then it seemed far away. Too far away to be of any concern. In the next instant, Derek was floating. Looking down on himself. The fragments of glass littering the floor glinted like stars beside his body. Then the room rotated and he was back on the floor again. In some ways, he still felt separated from his body. His limbs were numb. The pain that racked his trunk was too intense to withstand – his mind had detached itself from it. There was a bloodstain down the front of his lab coat but he had no idea where it had come from.

Mark was lying flat on the floor now. Viscous red blood had dribbled from the corner of his mouth to collect on the white floor of the laboratory. Derek levered himself into more of a sitting position. "Mark's dead," he said weakly. "It must be a great relief for Richards."

The ghostly reply from the hidden speaker seemed to Derek to echo around the lab, bombarding him from every side. "We did not expect such a rapid deterioration."

"Don't worry," he replied. "I'll give you entertainment for a bit yet."

There was a pause before the voice sounded again. "We did offer you alternatives, remember."

"What about your immune rabbits? Were they unaffected or did they suffer first and recover later?"

"They suffered. But . . ." The voice stopped.

"But not as much as this?"

"How do you feel?"

"What do you think? As if I could live forever."

Derek looked around the lab. Mark's body was as much a stain on the whiteness of the room as the blood was on Derek's white coat. It should be the other way round, Derek thought. This laboratory is a stain around Mark. It had been built in white to give the impression of cleanliness and purity but in fact it was corrupt and evil.

"Can you turn off the air supply from out there?" he asked.

"Yes."

"Good."

"Are you asking us to turn it off?"

No immune rabbit could have lived through this. It would have died of fright. He remembered Richards saying that Ellen and Jack had been sedated before death. Now Derek also wanted the easy option. No. Not easy. The only option. To do nothing was unbearable. "Yes. That's what I'm asking. Tell Richards not to worry," he added. "I haven't got natural immunity. His worries are over."

Derek tried to cling to his store of memories as his mind wandered, but he could not concentrate. As soon as he focused on and recognized one image, it drifted away – replaced by an uncontrolled succession of confused evocations. The disease had plundered and jumbled his memories, reducing them to shredded photographs. The scraps were falling through his fingers and those that he managed to grasp made no sense. He could not piece together the one image he longed to see. There were so few memories of her to draw on anyway. The last images drained away and he was left with nothing but a simple phrase that filled his mind. "Separation almost before we've started."

Derek's head turned slowly and painfully towards the microphone. A croaky voice that he would not have recognized as his own whispered, "Tell Sylvia . . ." Then his head fell onto his chest.

deprived of Derek and Derek had been deprived of her. But it was more than that. It was the worst type of loneliness. Because she had a secret that no one else in the world shared – outside the confines of the MoD. It segregated her from all others.

Had it been her fault? She could not bear a grudge against Mark. He loved her and was doing what he thought was right. She could not blame Derek. He had sacrificed himself to save thousands. And not one of those thousands even knew. To them, Derek was an absent-minded academic who had made a mistake when showing a schoolboy acquaintance round the university. A mistake that was responsible for Mark's and his own death. The press had cast him as the villain, not the hero. So who could she blame? Crookland Bay Research Station, certainly. And what about those CAR protesters? They had taken the dog's carcass in the first place. But it had not started with them. It had started with Paul Tedder encouraging the break-in. Like Mark, Paul Tedder had impeccable motives but the power of officialdom corrupted even the best intentions. With such power it was easy to pass the blame. At least till all the blameless were dead. Who else was at fault? Sylvia herself. If she had been honest with Mark, if she had told him straight that it was over between them, as their adolescent pact required her to do, there would have been no reason for him to go in search of glory to impress her. She hadn't told him for two reasons. Guilt. Instinct told her that to have an affair with her tutor was wrong. She was ashamed to admit to it. And insecurity. If Derek's fondness for her had happened to be her own girlish imaginings, she might have needed Mark to turn to. She had kept him hanging on as first reserve. It was her fault, too, that she and Derek became so entangled. He had resisted it but she had thrust herself upon him. Without that, perhaps Mark would not have been so resentful. Perhaps . . .

There was a knock at the door and her mother came in. "A letter for you," she said. "From the university."

"Thanks. I'll read it later."

"How are you feeling?"

Sylvia just shrugged in reply. Her mother sat beside her on the bed saying, "Want to tell me?"

Sylvia did not know what she wanted. To tell someone was the only way to allay her utter loneliness, but anyone she told would be threatened, as she was, by the awesome official conspiracy that she had witnessed. To keep it to herself, though, ended all resistance to the work carried out at Crookland Bay Research Centre. Neither Derek nor Mark, she felt, would want that. But she could not yet look to the future. She didn't have the motivation. When her numbness was replaced by remorse or anger, forgiveness or bitterness, then she would have the tools to react to the present and create a future for herself. For the moment, there was nothing. And she could not bear to talk about Derek and Mark. Not to her mother – not to anyone. She looked at her mum and shook her head. "No. I can't."

"Okay." Mrs Cooper put her hand fondly on Sylvia's leg. "Okay. I'm just sorry, Sylvia. Sorry for everything."

Sylvia nodded. "I'd better look at that letter now."

"Sure." Her mother got up and left the room.

The envelope bore the university insignia. She ripped it open and found inside a letter and another envelope. "Dear Miss Cooper," she read, "I enclose a letter that was found in Dr Thorn's office after his accident. As you can see, it is addressed to you and clearly Dr Thorn intended that you should receive it. After consulting the Head of Department, it was decided to send it on to you." The letter went on to tell her that she had been assigned a new personal tutor who was anxious to arrange a talk with her. The course director who had written the note added that the whole department was deeply saddened by Dr Thorn's death and that he knew how shocked she must be, considering her close relationship with her tutor. He ended with a sympathetic, optimistic wish that she might soon put it all behind her.

She put the letter down and picked up the other envelope. Her name and address were not typed, but handwritten by Derek. She held it for a minute before opening the envelope with fumbling fingers.

Dear Sylvia,

I promised that you would hear from me, whatever happened, so I write this just in case, hoping you never have to receive it. Tomorrow I'm going to work to face Mark and the T42. It makes it sound like a confrontation between me and Mark, doesn't it? It isn't, of course, but Richards has engineered it cleverly. The MoD's role can easily be made invisible to the public. Mine and Mark's can't. If the worst comes to the worst, Mark and I will carry the can. Nothing to do with the MoD.

By writing this letter I am trying to come to terms with what could happen tomorrow and, if the worst happens, to offer a few thoughts to you. I also want to cling a little longer to what would then be my last thread to you. I could write all night for that reason. God knows why I'm writing this "just in case" and "if the worst comes to the worst" stuff. It has come to the worst if you're reading this. One way or another, I've made a mess of it. I must write the remainder of this letter under the assumption that I get exposed to T42.

It's not easy to prepare myself for tomorrow when I hate so much what I'm getting drawn into.

I look calm enough now and I'll look calm enough tomorrow. I'll act calm enough as well, no doubt. As you know, that's the way I am. But inside, it's different. I can't work out exactly why I'm seething inside. It could be because of Richards, T42 and the rest of it, but more likely it's because of us. You and me. My Head of Department, your mum and Mark all tried to prise us apart. In the long term they all would have failed, I'm sure. Yet Richards, who is not interested in us as people – in people at all, maybe – will have succeeded. Damn him. At least I know how hurt Mark must be at losing you – now I am too. I am very sorry for him.

Another thing is bugging me. It's about Richards' intentions for tomorrow. If Mark and I had lived, what would the MoD have done with us? Especially Mark. We would have been an embarrassment, to say the least. It is so much cleaner for Richards for it to end as it has done. Could it be that he hoped for and planned this end? Or am I imposing villainy where it doesn't exist? Maybe simply disarming Mark and rendering the T42 safe would be his ideal conclusion. I don't know. I don't think I want to know the answer to this and it's best that you and I will never know.

Enough of Richards. What about me and my actions? I hope you understand them. I don't feel any need to justify them to anyone but you, and you are so close that I probably don't need to anyway. Since you are reading this letter, Mark and I have not survived, but I can't have made a complete hash of it. I must have contained the T42 – prevented its widespread release – otherwise there would be no one around to forward my letter to you. Protecting the public is my only reason for opposing Mark. I agree with him in every other way. I am not taking him on because of the clash over you. In that department, I have been altogether too successful for Mark's good. I feel regret for him, not malice. I am scared by the malice he probably feels for me.

Sorry if this letter jumps around a bit. I am trying to keep pace with all my thoughts and they are jumping around such a lot. They do keep coming back to you and me, though. When we first started meeting socially, I just took it at face value. The proverbial Platonic relationship, I thought. Or maybe I didn't think at all. I should have done. I should at least have considered the effect of our friendship on you. Your fellow students obviously thought there was more between us than friendship. Perhaps you did too. Even the Head of Department called it an improper relationship, as I recall. It was only me who was backward.

It was Ellen's death that really made me question where we were going. Don't get me wrong. You were never a substitute for Ellen. Maybe it's more accurate to say that you more than filled the big hole left by Ellen. *Much* more. No one gets to my age without seeing something of the opposite sex. I was neither young nor innocent when we got serious, but I might as well have been. Other women never made me feel like you did. They never really clicked with me, nor I with them. I'm sorry, Sylvia, I shouldn't go on like this. You know how I feel about you without me putting it in writing. I can only be making matters worse for you. You must forget and forgive. You won't believe it at the moment, but you have a bright future. It is the future you must think of, not the past. Remember, optimism is just one of your strong points.

What of the future? Well, personal recriminations won't help. If there's to be bitterness, it should be about the situation that arose, not just about one person. It's the situation that should be despised and fought, not just Richards – and certainly not Mark.

You should not despise chemistry either. It's a great subject. One institution's abuse of chemistry can't be allowed to sully the whole topic. If you want to prevent the situation from arising again, you must not give up on chemistry. Remember that once I told you that there were a couple of organizations working quietly and methodically out of the public eye to eliminate animal experiments? You have it in you to do much the same with chemical warfare. Fighting it from within, as they say. You have something for chemistry that is like green fingers in gardening. If you really want to compensate for your loss and have a real effect on chemical warfare, if you still feel strongly enough, do something that circumstances (and Richards) did not allow me to do. It will require hard work. That's good for you right now. A good degree, a doctorate and on to a research post. I'm sure you can do it if you want to. I have no need to instruct you in the type of research that would allow you to have an impact in the long term. It will become clear to you as you learn. Take care, though. Richards will have his policemen friends watching you for a while. Their memories will be fading by the time you are ready to start your research.

Now I need some way of finishing this letter. I wish I had all the time in the world to dream it up, but I don't. I must get some sleep even though it means losing that thread. I am sorry that your personal tutor let you down. Some knight in shining armour I turned out to be!

Be happy,

With all my love,
Derek.

Sylvia put down Derek's letter and went over to the window. Her tears rolled down as freely as the

Other titles by Malcolm Rose . . .

The Obtuse Experiment

What happens when the holiday of a lifetime turns into a nightmare you can't escape? In this tense thriller 350 "unsettled" schoolchildren embark on a trip to the Arctic Circle – but as the terrible truth behind the OBTUSE experiment becomes clear, they realize that they are all in grave danger . . .

Son of Pete Flude

Seb Flude has a lot to cope with – having a rock star father is not all it's cracked up to be. Girls for example – Seb never knows whether they're interested in him, or whether he's just an introduction to his sex-symbol dad! But when his rock 'n' roll connections lead to Seb's unwitting involvement in drug-smuggling, kidnapping and violence, things take an altogether more serious turn . . .

The Smoking Gun

When David Rabin is found dead in the school playing field, his sister Ros is determined to find the murderer. What is the connection with the sinister Dearing Scientific Laboratories? And what of the "smoking gun" – the lethal poison which killed David? Ros *must* find out, before she too becomes a victim . . .

Flight 116 is Down

The noise began.

Noise like an electric guitar stuck on one note, while the acoustics engineer turned the volume up, and up, and up, and up. A thrumming single note that sucked in the world.

The noise expanded like a planet exploding.

Like war.

A wind with the force of a fire truck's hose lifted her hair right out of the hood of her tied-tight jacket. One of her mittens was actually sucked off her hand. Her scream she could feel in her throat, but not hear; she was deaf; the entire world was screaming.

It was huge and black. A flying saucer, a nuclear bomb, a tornado on its side.

It was in her yard, in her rose garden.

Heidi's scream threw her to her knees.

Hostilities

"Dad!" Sharon shouted. "Oh, Dad, here I am!"

"Who's this?" His voice sounded confused.

"It's *me*. Sharon. I'm not lost at all. I'm not far from the car park."

"What? You want to speak to Sharon?"

"Dad! I'm here. Why don't you send someone to get me? It's *freezing* –" She stopped, because his voice had gone away from the receiver. He was calling from the kitchen phone up the stairwell. She could picture home so clearly from the echoes his voice made.

"Sharon!" She heard the distant words. "One of your weird friends is on the phone playing tricks. Are you in bed yet?..."

"*Daddy!*" Sharon shrieked in the phone box. This time her voice rang and echoed. Then she heard the other voice, coming through the receiver: "Hi."

"Who are you?" Sharon asked, bewildered.

"Sharon, of course."

"What do you mean? *I'm* Sharon!"

There was a laugh on the other end of the phone that turned for a second into a roaring sound as if an avalanche of stones had plunged on to the telephone box. Then the mocking voice came to Sharon's ear again. "*I'm* Sharon now."

FORBIDDEN

Without discussion, they began dancing. The music was slow, soaring with violins. The shadows elongated Daniel's dark features. He looked proud and mysterious.

In her white gauze and bright jewelry, Annabel glittered. Daniel touched her earrings and made them swing. They were tiny cats suspended in repeating circles of gold. He seemed mesmerized by the pendulum action.

Look at me, not my jewelry, Annabel willed him.

He looked at her.

She recognized him.

Her friend Emmie had been boasting about him for weeks.

He was Daniel Madison Ransom.

Secret Lives

"Who's the big Maori guy?" asked Beth in a dead flat voice as she made coffee for Brenda. "Haven't seen him much round here before except up the back in some of our classes."

"Bruno. Bruno Petrie. You don't see him much. He's an adult student. He shouldn't be allowed back here in the first place. He's not all that much older'n any of us and he's bad news. You name it and he's done it. They should never have let him back – he's violent."

"Where does he live?" asked Beth, even more flatly and quietly.

Brenda looked at Beth and Beth knew she had asked one question too many. "Out by you. You must've seen him. He's got an old motorbike he rides and you see him with a gun over his shoulder," she shuddered. "Up that old road just before Stella's, right up the top. Lives with his old man who's half loopy or dead or something. God knows why he came back to school. You'd never guess what he did when he was here last time..."

Seventeenth Summer

The long-haired man was introducing someone else, a girl. Penn's interest quickened. She was thin and frail-looking, with enormous sad eyes and long, straight, silver-blonde hair. Her voice was very clear, almost shrill, with a sadness that went with her looks.

> "Ten thousand miles it is too far
> To leave me here alone
> Here I may lie, lament and cry. . ."

Penn stopped scowling, transfixed by the sword-edge of the girl's voice. He had never seen a bird as perfect as this one, so utterly desirable. She was like a piece of crystal, delicate, brittle, rare. He had never seen one like it. All the girls he knew were busty and thrusty and strong, all private giggles and shrieks, nudging and daring and passing notes. They had no reticence, brash and sniggering. But this little wispy thing, like a puff of breeze, her voice full of tears . . . Penn's eyes were wide open, hypnotized. When she was finished he could not say anything. Bates looked at him and scowled.

He could not get her out of his head.

Point Horror

Read if you dare. . . .

Are you hooked on horror? Are you thrilled by fear? Then these are the books for you. A powerful series of horror fiction designed to keep you quaking in your shoes.

Also in the Point Horror series:

Mother's Helper
by A. Bates

April Fools
The Lifeguard
Teacher's Pet
Trick or Treat
by Richie Tankersley Cusick

My Secret Admirer
by Carol Ellis

Funhouse
The Accident
The Invitation
The Window
The Fever
The Train
by Diane Hoh

Thirteen
by Christopher Pike, R.L. Stine and others

Beach Party
The Baby-sitter
The Baby-sitter II
The Boyfriend
The Snowman
The Girlfriend
Hit and Run
Beach House
The Hitchhiker
by R.L. Stine

The Cheerleader
The Return of the Vampire
The Perfume
by Caroline B. Cooney

The Waitress
by Sinclair Smith

The Cemetery
by D.E. Athkins

P●INT CRiME

If you like Point Horror, you'll love Point Crime!

A murder has been committed . . . Whodunnit?
Was it the teacher, the schoolgirl, or the best friend? An exciting new series of crime novels, with tortuous plots and lots of suspects, designed to keep the reader guessing till the very last page.

School for Death
Peter Beere
When the French teacher is found, drowned in the pond, Ali and her friends are plunged into a frightening nightmare. Murder has come to Summervale School, and *anyone* could be the next victim . . .

Shoot the Teacher
David Belbin
Adam Lane, new to Beechwood Grange, finds himself thrust into the middle of a murder investigation, when the headteacher is found shot dead. And the shootings have only just begun . . .

The Smoking Gun
Malcolm Rose
When David Rabin is found dead, in the school playing-field, his sister Ros is determined to find the murderer. But who would have killed him? And why?

Look out for:

Baa Baa Dead Sheep
Jill Bennett
Mr Lamb, resident caretaker of the *Tree Theatre*, has been murdered, and more than one person at the theatre had cause to hate him . . .

Avenging Angel
David Belbin
When Angelo Coppola is killed in a hit-and-run accident, his sister, Clare, sets out to find his killer . . .